BILL DOYLE

CRIME THROUGH TIME™
BETRAYED!

THE 1977 JOURNAL OF ZEKE MOORIE

LITTLE, BROWN AND COMPANY
New York ᐧ Boston ᐧ London

Cover illustration by Steve Cieslawski
Interior illustrations by Brian Hoskins
Back cover and title page illustration by Brian Dow
Designed by Atif Toor and Mark Weinberg
Photos: pp. 12, 59/Ablestock; p. 56/Atif Toor; p. 70/Library of Congress; p.141/Riccardo Salmona
The Inspector photos: p. 1/Barry Sweet/Zuma Press/Newscom; p. 2 (top left, top right)/Ablestock,
(center)/Library of Congress, (bottom left)/OAR/National Undersea Research Program
(NURP)/NOAA, (bottom right)/NASA Marshall Space Flight Center (NASA-MSFC);
p. 3 (top)/Paramount Pictures/Zuma Press/Newscom, (bottom)/Lucas Film Ltd./Zuma
Press/Newscom; p. 4 (top, center right)/KPA/Zuma Press/Newscom, (center left, bottom)/Ablestock

Little, Brown and Company

1271 Avenue of the Americas, New York, NY 10020
Visit our Web site at www.lb-kids.com

First Edition: July 2006

Library of Congress Cataloging-in-Publication Data

Doyle, Bill H., 1968–
    Betrayed! 1977 : the journal of Zeke Moorie / Bill Doyle.—1st ed.
        p. cm. — (Crime through time)
  Summary: While working for a traveling disco show accompanying the King Tut exhibition in 1977,
fourteen-year-old Zeke investigates a series of mishaps involving the cast and crew, mysterious mes-
sages, centuries-old artifacts, and an ancient curse.
  ISBN 0-316-05741-X (trade pbk.)
  [1. Ciphers—Fiction. 2. Disco dancing—Fiction. 3. Dancing—Fiction. 4. Egypt—Antiquities—
Fiction. 5. United States—History—1969—Fiction. 6. Mystery and detective stories.] I. Title. II.
Series: Doyle, Bill H., 1968– Crime through time.
  PZ7.D7725Bet 2006
  [Fic]—dc22   2005021539

CW

10 9 8 7 6 5 4 3 2 1

Printed in the United States of America

ACKNOWLEDGMENTS

A thank-you of historic proportions to Nancy Hall for making this book and the Crime Through Time series a reality. To Kirsten Hall for her insightful grasp of the overall picture, to Linda Falken for her skillful editing and amazing eagle-eye for detail, and to Atif Toor for bringing the books alive visually.

Special thanks to the editors at Little, Brown: Andrea Spooner, Jennifer Hunt, Phoebe Sorkin, and Rebekah Rush McKay, who are always dead-on, always incisive, and never discouraging. And thanks to Riccardo Salmona for his constant support.

Our old school bus felt more like a roasting pan!

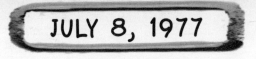

JULY 8, 1977

3:25 PM

A mummy is right behind me!

It feels weird to write that in my journal, but it's true. An ancient Egyptian pharaoh is following our bus as we rumble down Highway 55 toward New Orleans.

But I'd bet my favorite Donna Summer record that the mummy's having a much better trip than I am. The pharaoh is cruising along in a heavily guarded truck that has air-conditioning to protect his 3,300-year-old body from decay. And special shock absorbers to keep the fifty priceless items from his tomb from bouncing around.

Can't say the same about our ride. Each pebble we run over sends a giant jolt through the old school bus. The springs poking out of the cheap vinyl seats are jabbing into my backside. And forget about pleasant temperatures—unless you like the desert. Even with all the windows open, the summer sun is cooking us like bugs in a can.

At first, the other twenty kids on board didn't seem to notice. They were too busy being yelled at by the dance instructor, Madame Katerina. She rocked back and forth in the aisle, her plump body wedged between two seats. Everything about her is fierce: from her extremely tight orange headscarf to the way she slams down the end of her ballet stick when she's upset.

Madame Katerina

"Attention, you, my babies!" she shouted, her Russian accent rising above the clanking of the bus and the rushing wind. "First off," she said, "you are most laziest of all dancers in world!"

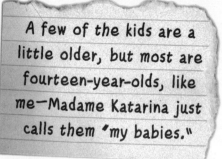

A few of the kids are a little older, but most are fourteen-year-olds, like me—Madame Katarina just calls them "my babies."

She pressed a button on the 8-track tape player on the seat next to her. "Listen to this and concentrate," she ordered as the sweaty air filled with the hot new disco tunes of the Bee Gees.

"1, 2, 3 . . . 4! 1, 2, 3 . . . 4!" she repeated over and over, ramming her stick down in rhythm. I could hear the kids going through the steps of the dance around me. She gave each of them a long, scrutinizing look as if she could see their feet moving under the bench seats. I tried tapping my foot in time to the music, but it jerked around like a remote-control toy gone haywire. My brain just wasn't sending down the right signals, and I gave up.

Okay, I'm a detective—not a dancer. So luckily, I didn't have to pay attention to Madame Katerina and could check out the scenery zipping by outside my window.

There were actually people out there lining the sides of the highway! They were cheering as our bus rattled by. Little kids sat on their parents' shoulders, waving their hands and shouting. It's like I'm traveling with The Fonz or Mark Spitz. As I looked at the starstruck faces, it was clear to me that America had fallen head over heels for the mummy in the truck behind our bus—King Tut.

TUT-TUT, HOREMHEB

The Egyptian pharaoh King Tutankhamen—better known as King Tut—was born around 1341 BCE His name means "the living image of Aten," who was a god worshiped by ancient Egyptians. Tut took the throne when he was only eight or nine years old and was already married to a girl of about the same age. At the time, Egypt was a superpower, and the boy ruled over as many as 1.5 million people. Tut's reign was short, ending when he died at eighteen or nineteen. A later pharaoh, Horemheb, wanted to be the only ruler that the Egyptians remembered and tried to wipe out traces of Tut's existence. But by hiding Tut's tomb, Horemheb protected it from grave robbers and ensured that it would be discovered almost completely intact thousands of years later. In other words, because Horemheb wanted him forgotten, Tut will be remembered forever.

A bunch of Tut's fans were holding up signs. They read:

KING TUT (STILL) RULES!

I'M A TUT MANIAC!

I LOVE THE PHARAOH MORE THAN MY CAMARO!

The signs helped make me feel like I was part of something important. I was just starting to think that maybe clattering along in this sauna with wheels all summer was worth it.

And then—

BEWARE!!!
THE MUMMY'S CURSE!

The letters of this last sign dripped with thick black paint. It was held by a grim-looking man wearing a dirty sweat suit. Even in the heat, I felt a chill run down my spine.

HOW TO AVOID THE CURSE!

What does the curse say?
Anyone who disturbs the tomb of King Tut will come to an untimely end!

This scary idea was made popular by Marie Corelli—a Scottish fiction writer. And later, Hollywood movies made the curse seem more real!

What happens?
According to an inscription on a brick in the tomb: "I will destroy all those who cross this threshold into the sacred rooms of the royal king who lives forever."

It doesn't really say this. A better translation is: "I am the one who keeps the sand from blocking this secret chamber."

Who are the victims . . . so far?
• Lord Carnarvon, who financed the dig, died. (His son said the family dog howled and then died at the same time as his master—but the dog was hundreds of miles away!)

Carnarvon died seven weeks after the opening of the burial chamber from an infection he got by shaving over a mosquito bite on his face.

• A scientist on his way to the dig site died.

• An Egyptian prince living in London murdered his wife.

But neither of these people ever even visited King Tut's tomb!

• And many others!

Lots of deaths and misfortunes were blamed on the curse.

No one else on the bus seemed to notice, and I turned to look again, but the man had already disappeared as we rounded a turn. I shook off the weird feeling—I'm normally too practical to be affected by superstition. It must be that I've never left Nebraska before, and I'm feeling a little homesick for Mom and Dad.

Mom and Dad

They are staying at home on our cattle ranch outside Omaha, while my twin brother, R.T., and I are spending our summer vacation on the road. We've been hired by TEENS FOR TUT, a disco television show that travels from city to city with the King Tut exhibition.

Maybe "hired" is the wrong word. Sure, we do tons of work—R.T.'s a dancer, and I work behind the scenes—but we don't get paid or anything. Mr. Myles, the producer of the show, says we get to see the country and spread the joy of entertainment—what do we need with money? Out of the goodness of his heart, he will feed us and provide a room in one of the trailers.

After school let out for the summer, the cast and crew met in St. Louis. We rehearsed there for a week before heading off to New Orleans for our first show.

What do I know about disco? Not much. This whole thing was my brother's idea. He told Mr. Myles he wouldn't go unless they invited me along, too.

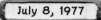

TEENS FOR TUT PRODUCTIONS
St. Louis, Missouri 57478

May 3, 1977
Dr. and Mrs. Randall Moorie
Rural Route #4
Hartland, Nebraska 54393

Dear Dr. and Mrs. Moorie,

Congratulations! Your son R.T. has been accepted to
dance in the chorus of Teens for Tut! Please sign
the enclosed legally binding contract and follow the
attached directions to our first rehearsal in St. Louis.

Yours in Disco,

Nathaniel Myles

Mr. Nathaniel J. Myles, Producer

P.S. Per your son's "take it or leave it" request, we
are willing "to take" your other son, Zeke. I suppose
we'll find something for him to do backstage.

That last part of the letter is about me. That's the way
it usually goes with R.T. and me—he's the star. Most people
would think I'd be jealous of him. But I'm not jealous—
curious is a better description. I mean, how can twins be
so different?

My brother is tall, handsome, athletic, a great dancer—
and I'm . . . well, I'm not. Back home he'll jump on a horse
that's just been broken that day and ride it bareback.
And I still like the pony, Teddy, I got when I was eight.

R.T.'s a great guy, though, and would never rub my face in it. If anything, he says he's jealous of me. He thinks I ended up with all the brains. "I'd kill to be able solve cases the way you and Dad do," he told me once when I was feeling sorry for myself. Dad is an expert at detecting scams and cons. "I'd love to be like you, Enigma."

It's true cryptanalysis just comes naturally to me. At times, I find myself slipping into what our family friend Judge Pinkerton calls the Code Zone. The way some people just look up into the sky and see clouds, I can look at something—the bricks of a building or words on a page—and suddenly, I see numbers, codes, and hidden patterns.

R.T. calls me "enigma" sometimes because the Enigma was a code machine used in World War II, and I'm so good at breaking and writing codes.

11

Say I just glance at a pineapple—I'll feel something like a little itch at the back of my brain and then— BLAM! I'm in the Code Zone and the numbers 8 and 13 pop out at me.

In pineapples and pinecones, it's easy to spot two different kinds of spirals. One running clockwise, has 13 spirals, and the other in the opposite direction, has 8 spirals. IT'S ALWAYS THE SAME!

Like everyone in my family, R.T.'s a good detective, too. But his specialty is a little more social. He's better at figuring out what makes people happy—and he loves telling jokes.

In fact, he's telling one right now. Madame Katerina has stopped yelling at the dancers and is talking to Mr. Myles at the front of the bus—so R.T. is setting up the punch line to a joke.

"That's when the duck says to the pharaoh, he says . . ." R.T. is slapping his forehead as if trying to remember how it ends. The kids around him are hanging on his every word as if he's telling them the meaning of life. Uh-oh. R.T. just turned toward me, pushing back his thick blonde hair. I know what's coming next . . .

"Hey, Enigma, what's the punch line?"

The other kids looked at me and waited for me to say something. But I just stared back.

R.T.'s smile dipped slightly with worry. He was just trying to include me, and it was going wrong. "You know . . . that duck joke?" he prodded me gently. "How's it go?"

"I . . . I . . . ," I stammered. I couldn't think. Attention like that makes me freeze up. I get stage fright and my mind goes blank.

Come on! COME ON! I shouted at myself.

"The duck says . . ." My voice trailed off into nervous silence. How could I be so smart about tough things and so dumb about this simple stuff? I felt pathetic. R.T. gave me a wink, which meant, "No big deal. Don't worry about it."

Snapping his fingers, he said to everyone else, "I remember! The duck says to the pharaoh, 'I sphinx, therefore I am!'"

The other kids laugh and slap R.T. on the back like it was the funniest thing they'd ever heard. Thanks to him, they're already forgetting about how stupid I acted.

"We love you, King Tut!" a woman standing by the road just shouted at the bus.

Great, I thought. Nothing like traveling with a 3,300-hundred-year-old mummy who is better with people than you are to really build your confidence!

Food tables were set up in the parking lot.

JULY 9, 1977

3:25 PM

This morning, I woke up at seven o'clock in the tiny room I share with R.T. There was no morning sun streaming through the windows—because there were no windows!

Our room is like a closet with a bunk bed (R.T. gets the top, I get the bottom). We use the bus to travel from city to city, but at night, we climb aboard one of the two trailers. Each one has been split into seven mini bedrooms, giving the twenty-eight members of the cast and crew a place to sleep.

Yesterday, the whole caravan—including the two trucks that carried King Tut and his treasures—pulled into the back parking lot of the New Orleans History Museum. It's kind of like camping out—if your campground was a big, greasy concrete slab where cars usually park. But not everyone has to stay here. After Tut's treasures are safely loaded into the museum, the guards who watch over the exhibit while it's on the road get to stay in fancy hotels.

When a few of the kids in the TEENS FOR TUT had complained that this was unfair, Mr. Myles just shrugged and said, "But you kids get the applause after the show! That's worth more than all the hotel rooms in the world."

The show! My heart skipped a few beats when I realized we had a television show to do in just a few hours.

From my bunk, I kicked the bottom of R.T.'s thin mattress to wake him up. He mumbled something, and I could hear him turn over and start snoring again.

I decided to get going without him. After changing into my cut-off jeans and my favorite T-shirt (the one that says SWEET!), I squeezed out the door.

The sun had just come up, but you could tell it was going to be a scorcher. Most of the dancers were already up and hovering around two long tables that had been set up near the bus. Madame Katerina darted here and there in a flurry of activity as she organized breakfast. The tables were heaped with all sorts of fruits, doughnuts, muffins, juices, and other treats.

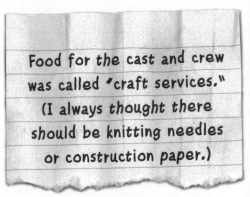

Food for the cast and crew was called "craft services." (I always thought there should be knitting needles or construction paper.)

I walked over and reached for a strawberry pastry (my favorite), and out of nowhere, a hand slapped mine. It was Madame Katerina. She said, "No! You are crew. Dancers eat the first. Then you!"

Embarrassed, I took a step back and waited for the other kids to fill their plates. Everyone seemed nervous and on edge. I guess it's because the show was scheduled for 3:00 in the afternoon. That only gave them seven hours to get ready.

And it's not like I didn't have anything to do. I'm the production assistant or P.A. It's my job to do . . . well, everything that no one else wants to do. Like making sure the dancers are ready to go onstage, that all the props are set and working, that Mr. Myles's cup of coffee is made with six packets of sugar.

By the time it was my turn to go through the line, all that was left was a squashed banana and a crumbled piece of toast.

Madame Katerina grabbed the banana before I could and tossed it on another boy's plate. "Dancers must be strong and vital to perform," she told the boy. "Especially since my Muse came to me last night!"

"No, not your Muse!" The boy with my banana cried, and a few of the other kids groaned.

Madame Katerina claimed to be in contact with the Muse of Dance, who visited her dreams. When Madame Katerina got a visit, the dance was usually drastically altered.

"Yes, is right," Madame Katerina said fiercely. "The Muse demands the dance must be changed."

"That's not fair," a tall chorus dancer whined through a mouthful of apple. "We've been working on that dance for weeks, and the show is in just a few hours!"

Madame Katerina turned toward her. "I will not stand for—"

She broke off as R.T. emerged from the trailer. He must have snuck two cinnamon buns from dinner last night—he was always hoarding food. Now, he held them up to his ears like Princess Leia from that new sci-fi movie STAR WARS.

R.T. kidding around

With the buns to his ears, he announced, "Boy, break-fast SOUNDS so good!"

Okay, the joke definitely isn't funny when I write it down here in my journal, but the way R.T. says things, they can be really hilarious.

Everyone laughed, even Madame Katerina. But she quickly got back to business. "Enough games!" she bellowed, whapping her stick on the ground. "Now is work time. All dancers come with me over to end of parking lot, and I will show you new dance steps from my Muse. You in crew, time for work."

With another group groan, the dancers followed her across the lot. R.T walked by me, munching on one of his "ears." He said, "See you later, Enigma."

"See you," I said and headed into the museum to get to work.

Stage

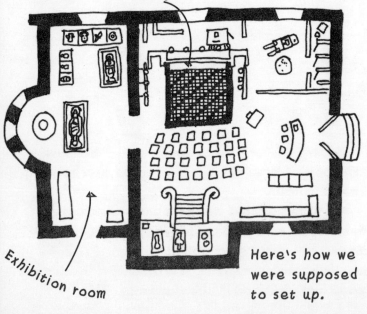

Exhibition room

Here's how we were supposed to set up.

The auditorium where the show would be held was a disaster. Crates, pipes, ropes, lights, everything was scattered across the stage. I walked over to two burly guys, and they put me to work helping to assemble the dance floor.

The dance performance takes place on a giant mobile disco floor. The floor is made up of 225 different-colored boxes. Each box contains a light bulb that lights up when a dancer steps on it. The floor looks like this:

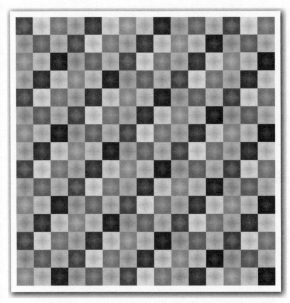

Our floor looks like the one from the movie SATURDAY NIGHT FEVER, but it's different. With ours, dancers light the boxes by stepping on them.

Two hours later, we had the floor set up. The burly guys took a coffee break, and I headed over to the drinking fountain.

Mr. Myles spotted me there and stormed over. His mousy secretary, Lucy, followed on his heels. "Hey, buster!" Mr. Myles sputtered at me—it was clear he couldn't remember my name. "I'm not paying you to stand around and drink water. Come with me."

19

I wanted to point out that he wasn't PAYING me at all. But instead, I followed him backstage. We passed the prop area and the costume racks and ended up next to a forklift.

"See that sand?" Mr. Myles asked me, pointing at a giant barrel filled with sand on the front end of the forklift. "I want you to put it in those bags." He gestured toward a stack of empty canvas sacks that sat on a tarp-covered table nearby. "Got it?"

"You want me to make sandbags?" I said.

"You're a genius, kid," Mr. Myles said sarcastically.

Probably trying to soften his tone, Lucy cut in. She spoke in a flat voice, almost a monotone. "We tie the bags to the ends of ropes, and the bags' weight helps us raise and lower the lights and other equipment safely."

I nodded. I understood, but it seemed like they might put my brain to better use.

Mr. Myles must have read my thoughts. He looped an arm around my shoulder. "That's showbiz, kid. One day you're stuffing sandbags, the next your name is in lights." For a split second, his eyes went kind of dreamy. Then, just as quickly, he snapped out of it. "Why are you yammering on and on? I've got a show to run!" He hurried off to yell at someone else, and Lucy went chasing after him.

Well, it could be worse, I thought as I reached up to take a canvas bag and start filling it with sand. They could ask me to dance.

After about an hour of mind-numbing work, a voice bellowed, "Clear the way for his royal highness!" It was Richard King, a big bear of a man who was in charge of the lights for the show.

He had a bushy mustache, sprayed spit when he talked, and insisted that we reverse his name and call him King Richard—but I liked the guy. He lent me copies of his Sherlock Holmes mysteries to read on the bus, and he had a great sense of humor.

King Richard

He was leading Mr. Myles back over to the tarp-covered table. Richard took the remaining canvas sacks off the top and handed them to me. He turned to Mr. Myles.

"We need to buy our own equipment for this show. Look at this lighting booth!" He pulled back the tarp. And I saw that beneath it wasn't a high table at all, but a very small booth. "You expect me to use this to run the lights for the show?"

The booth was a rusting metal box with walls as high as my chin. It clearly had been built years ago for another long-forgotten purpose. Cables and wires snaked from holes drilled in the side of the booth, and a control panel had been welded to the interior. There was room for a chair, but it seemed impossible that Richard would ever fit inside.

"How cozy!" Mr. Myles said. "Why this booth looks excellent!"

But Richard wasn't buying it. "That's not the worst." He walked to the nearby wall and removed a huge steel plate,

21

revealing a snarl of coiled electrical wires. It looked like an old-age home for snakes—very dangerous snakes.

"Mr. Myles," Richard said, "this electrical system is older than King Tut. It can't keep up with the modern demands of 1970s disco."

Mr. Myles wiped the spray of Richard's saliva off his face with his handkerchief. "You say this every time we do a show, Richard. If you can't do it, I'll just have to get someone who can."

Mr. Myles

"I'm in the union, Mr. Myles," Richard said, but Mr. Myles's words had had the desired effect. Richard opened the steel door of the lighting booth, which had a little plastic window. He squeezed down into the chair and closed the door behind him. He looked like a huge sardine shoved into a too-small can. "You can't fire me," he said like a king on a throne—a very big king on a very tiny throne.

Mr. Myles lips twitched, and I could tell he was trying not to laugh. "Whatever you say, Richard! Just make it work," he said and rushed off.

While I filled bag after bag with sand, I watched King Richard do battle with the electrical system. For a big guy, he was a whirling dervish of arms, snipping wires and reconnecting cables. Three hours later, I was still stuffing sacks with sand when King Richard squished back into his booth and said out loud, "Here goes nothing."

He hit a button, and there was a low whirring sound. But from where I stood, I could see the dance floor suddenly come to life. King Richard *pumped* the air and shouted, "All hail the king!" He had the power up and running. And just in time.

"Two minutes until show time, people," Lucy called in her flat voice.

The huge barrel was still filled halfway with sand, but I had run out of sacks. I walked over to check out King Richard's handiwork as he continued to fine-tune things on his panel. As I gazed at the wires, there was that itch in the back of my brain, and I felt myself slip into the Code Zone.

The pattern was off. Something was wrong.

"Are you sure about that connection?" I asked him, pointing at the wires that sprouted in all directions and then disappeared into the wall. There was a blue cable in the mix that seemed out of place.

"Yes, I'm sure," he said gruffly, then gave me an apologetic smile. "Sorry, kid. King Richard is just a little hot and cranky. Save yourself from my royal wrath and go watch the show, would you?"

I smiled back and said, "Sure."

I walked closer toward the edge of the stage but was careful to stay behind the curtain so the live audience and the camera wouldn't be able to see me. I could hear the excited chatter of people as they took their seats for the show.

Out on the stage, the dancers were still rehearsing at the last second. Madame Katerina whizzed around them like an angry queen bee. She jammed her stick against the floor and shouted, "Remember! My Muse makes the demand that this dance be done exactly right."

23

"Sixty seconds!" Lucy called. "Dancers to your places. Madame Katerina, clear the floor."

The choreographer left, and I gave R.T. a wave to wish him good luck. He returned a salute.

There was a schedule of events on the wall near me.

SCHEDULE OF EVENTS:

① Guest Host Introduces Show

② Dance Extravaganza

③ Commercial Break

④ Meet King Tut (Pre-Recorded Video)

⑤ Commercial Break

⑥ Dancing (Egyptian) Queen

⑦ Secret Map Box and Dance Finale!

Each TEENS FOR TUT show opens with a local sponsor or businessperson introducing the show to the crowd. Today, a nervous man who owned a series of car dealerships stood before the camera. He was sweating through his silver polyester shirt and didn't seem to know what to do with his hands.

A cameraman held up three fingers and said, "And we go live in 3..., 2..." He brought down a finger with each new number—but the cameraman never said "1" just in case the camera had turned on early.

But I knew it hadn't. You can tell a camera is broadcasting by the light on top of it. If the light shines bright red, you know the camera is on.

And now the red light blinked on—and the show started. I imagined the tens of thousands of people across the country who would be tuning in to watch.

Lucy held up a sign that said APPLAUSE and the audience clapped and cheered.

The nervous man licked his dry lips as he read out loud from the cue cards behind the camera. "Ladies and gentlemen, travel back with me, if you will, to a time when mystery and magic ruled the Earth. Come journey with me over 3,000 years ago when a young pharaoh ruled the desert! And remember, when you want a chariot to drive you and your little pharaohs around the pyramids, come to Dickson's Auto Mart!" And the musicians on the other side of the stage started playing a Bee Gees hit. The man stood in the light for a second, looking confused about what to do next. Lucy signaled him to get off the stage.

Richard turned on the lights over the dance floor, and they burst into blinding-white life. The audience squinted and by the time their eyes had adjusted, my brother and the other dancers had taken their places on the floor.

Now the band switched to the hottest Bee Gees tune on the radio.

Without any help from Lucy, the audience started clapping. I'm surprised they didn't start laughing.

The dancers' costumes weren't like the ones KISS wears, but they were pretty ridiculous. Each dancer wore Egyptian robes and a mask. Max, the lead dancer—a sleek, good-looking kid from Miami—wore the funeral mask of King Tut. A tall chorus girl wore a jackal mask with a long snout. And R.T. was wearing the head of some kind of bird, which I didn't recognize. I doubt anyone in ancient Egypt would have, either.

R.T.'s mask

Max's mask

As the music got cranking, the lead dancer really started to move. There was lots of spinning, small kicks, and fancy footwork. Because Max was the lead, he hopped and spun in front of everyone else. The other twelve dancers were in the chorus and formed a pyramid behind him.

Max was a decent dancer, but I knew my brother was better. I could tell R.T. had to force himself not to jump higher or turn with more snap than Max. As Max strutted from one box on the floor to another, the lights under his feet blinked on and off in a spectacular display of colors.

It was strange, but as I watched them, I suddenly felt that familiar itch somewhere in the back of my mind—

POP!

The sound of a small explosion broke into my thoughts. The smell of burning wire filled the air as half the lights under the dance floor started flickering like crazy.

The musicians continued to play, and the dancers were doing their best to keep the show going—but the audience was looking around fearfully as if checking for the nearest emergency exit. I glanced back at the lighting booth where King Richard sat with a panicked look on his face.

"All the lights! They're too much for the system!" he cried, clearly not caring if the audience heard him above the music or not.

"The blue cable! Disconnect the blue one!" I called as loudly as I dared. I wondered if Richard had heard me. And then I had my answer, because the lights blazed back to life.

The sudden brightness seemed to blind many of the dancers. Two girls collided and bounced off each other. The kid wearing the Anubis costume fell back into the curtain and started thrashing around like a fly caught in glue. A girl

27

dressed as an Egyptian priestess and holding a scepter skidded across the stage. Only R.T. and Max managed to keep their feet under them.

Even in all the chaos, Max seemed determined to get to the end of the number. Madame Katerina's choreography called for the other dancers to lie down in a line and for Max to leap over them and land in a split.

But while most of the dancers were lying down, there was nothing orderly about them. They were sprawled every-where. Max looked more like a driver at the county fair about to jump over a bunch of wrecked cars. Only R.T. and the girl dressed as a priestess were in the right spot, lying on their backs in the middle of the stage. Max took a few steps back and launched himself into the air—

He didn't leap high enough, and the scepter of the priestess caught on the hem of his robe. It was just enough to throw him off-kilter. Max's body twisted in midair, and he went sailing into the audience. There were screams as he slammed

directly into an older man with dark hair and white sideburns in the front row.

There were more shocked cries from the audience—and even some laughter.

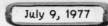

"Commercial! Go to commercial!" I heard Mr. Myles screaming. The red light above the camera finally went out. We were no longer broadcasting. People at home were now watching an ad rather than a bunch of kids with strange masks stumbling around the stage.

I rushed past the dance floor and out to the audience to see if I could help anyone. The man Max had catapulted into was crawling to his feet and straightening his glasses. The thick lenses made his eyes look like fish swimming in a tank, and he looked upset.

Max was still sprawled partially under a chair in the second row, his King Tut mask twisted around to the back of his head. I helped him up and turned back to the man with the glasses, but he was gone. R.T. stood in his place. My brother held his bird mask in one hand and reached out to steady Max with the other.

"Are you okay, Max?" I asked.

He nodded, looking dazed. "I think so," he said. "It's not my fault. Madame Katerina's dance was too hard. No one could do it."

I glanced at R.T. I knew he wanted to say, "I could." But instead, he said, "Come on, guys, let's help the others."

We were moving to do just that when a scream filled the air. "Oh, no!" It came from behind the curtain. "Help me—!" The voice broke off.

"Now what?" R.T. said as audience members started to get up from their seats.

"Please stay calm, everyone!" Lucy appeared out of nowhere and soothed the audience. "It's all part of the show."

29

But I knew it wasn't. That call had been full of very real fear and panic. Someone was hurt or in danger.

"Get to the pay phone outside the auditorium," I told R.T. "Call an ambulance!"

I rushed backstage. Once there, I found the strangest thing I've ever seen.

The screams had come from King Richard, and I could see why. He was still seated in the lighting booth—but he was no longer alone in the tight space.

I rubbed my eyes to make sure I wasn't having a nightmare.

A waterfall of sand was pouring down on top of him!

Somehow, the forklift had moved behind Richard's booth. The barrel of sand had been lifted up in the air directly over the booth, and the bottom had broken off. The heavy sand pouring out had crashed through the top of the booth and now, it was flowing all over Richard!

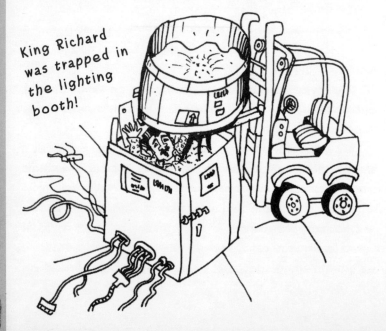

King Richard was trapped in the lighting booth!

The sand was already up to his shoulders, trapping him inside the booth—and soon his head would be buried.

He looked terrified. "Kid, get me out of here! I think I broke a rib!"

I darted to the door of the booth and yanked on the handle. But it wouldn't budge. The pressure of the sand from inside had bent the lock. I pushed on the booth itself, but it was bolted to the floor.

"I'm being buried alive!" Richard cried as he struggled to get free.

"Where are the keys to the forklift?" one of the two burly guys shouted. "I can't move it!"

Mr. Myles and Lucy must have been busy calming the audience. Max and a few of the other dancers stood there looking dumbfounded.

We had to do something!

I grabbed the jackal mask from the tall girl's hands—

"Hey!" she cried.

I shoved the mask over Richard's head just as the sand reached the level of his ears. The long snout of the mask stuck up out of the still-falling sand, like a snorkel sticking up out of water. It would let Richard breathe until we could figure something out.

R.T. strode over to the booth. He was carrying a crowbar. The tall chorus girl sighed at the heroic sight. R.T. wedged it in the crack of the door and put all his body weight behind it. The door flew open and, pushed by waves of sand, Richard popped out of the booth like a cork exploding from a bottle.

It took two big men to pull King Richard out of the booth.

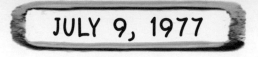

The two burly guys pulled King Richard out of the pile of sand.

"Ow!" he cried and clutched at his ribs. He looked like he might faint from the pain.

I moved closer to R.T. and asked in a low voice, "How did that barrel of sand get right over his head?"

R.T. shook his head. "I don't know, bro. You were the last one near it. Maybe the forklift rolled over here on its own? It looks pretty old."

"It rolled over on its own, lifted the barrel, and positioned it exactly over Richard's head?" I said. "And the barrel just happened to crack open? We need to secure this area. It could be a crime—"

Before I could say anything else, two paramedics brushed past us. They were wheeling a rattling stretcher between them. Relief swept over me. Medical help for Richard had arrived.

"You got here fast," R.T. said to them.

"Yeah, we were taking a break just around the corner when the call came in," one of them said.

"You don't charge extra for rush service, do you?" Mr. Myles asked them as he joined us. When Richard grunted in disgust, Mr. Myles held up his hands. "Just kidding, just kidding!"

Wearing a headset that kept her in touch with the control room, Lucy scurried over to Mr. Myles. Sure, she might look mousy—but she seemed to be the calmest one of any of us. "Boss," she told him. "We've had almost twenty minutes of commercials. What do you want to do?"

Mr. Myles took a look at the damage around him, and his eyes settled on me. "Run one more sixty-second commercial," he told Lucy. "We'll skip all the other dances and go back on the air for the Secret Map Box presentation."

Lucy spoke into her headset. "Sixty-second spot and then bring us back live." She said to Mr. Myles, "What about the spotlight for the Secret Map Box presentation?"

He said to me, "I've been watching you. You know about lights?"

I felt dazed. "What?"

"Forty-five seconds," Lucy announced calmly, sending the rest of the cast and crew into a tizzy of frantic movement.

A vein in Mr. Myles' temple started to pulse as he asked me again, "Do. You. Know. About. Lights?"

"Yeah, sure," I said. "I guess—"

"Good, you're in charge of the lights," he barked.

I fumbled for a response and looked down at Richard, who was now resting on a stretcher. His beet-red face was screwed up in pain, and the emergency team had placed an oxygen mask over it, but he managed to whisper, "The show must go on." He gave me a small smile as they wheeled him away on the stretcher.

I decided it'd be good for Richard to know his lights were in capable hands. "Okay, I'll do—" I started to tell Mr. Myles, but he wasn't listening.

"Lucy, come with me!" he said and headed back into the auditorium.

Before leaving, Lucy said, "Zeke, the spotlight operator will move the light where it needs to go. You just have to turn all the lights off except the spotlight, and you'll be fine." She turned to follow Mr. Myles and announced, "Fifteen seconds until we go back on the air."

I'll be fine? Less than fifteen seconds, and I had to find the cable for the spotlight, and the lighting booth was full of sand. And I'll be FINE?

My heart pounding, I worked quickly. There it was! The cable that controlled the spotlight. I had to remove it from the booth and plug it directly into the wall.

Just then, I heard the cameraman start his countdown. "And we're back in 3 . . ."

Mr. Myles was now standing in the center of the dark stage. I yanked on the cable, it was stuck!

"2 . . ."

The show was about to start in the dark!

Suddenly, the cable came free from the booth—

I imagined the cameraman silently making a "1" with his finger—

And I rammed it home.

The spot sprang to life at the exact same instant the camera's red light popped on.

Mr. Myles was normally a blustering, bellowing bundle of nerves, but when he stepped in front of the camera, he became a slick ringmaster.

"Ladies and gentlemen," he said, oozing charm. "I

apologize for tonight's performance. One might even say it was cursed . . ." This reference to the Mummy's Curse brought laughter and applause from the audience.

Mr. Myles waited for the noise to die down. "And now the portion of the evening that many of you have been waiting for!" He turned toward the other side of the stage. "Frank, if you please!"

The spotlight in the center of the stage widened, and Frank, the stoop-shouldered security guard, wheeled a cart into the circle of light. On top of the cart was a box that was about the size of a microwave oven. It was made of what looked to be alabaster and was covered in hieroglyphs— the writing of the ancient Egyptians.

Ripples of excitement washed over the audience.

"What on Earth is that thing?" A flat voice asked. It was Lucy. Mr. Myles had asked her to sit in the audience during this part of the show.

"Good question, little lady," Mr. Myles answered as if he didn't know her. "The Secret Map Box was found in the innermost chamber of King Tut's tomb. It was at the feet of the mummy—as if he might wake up at any point and want to look at it. There are hundreds of hieroglyphs on the box, which has five layers that turn. Archaeologists believe that if you line up the hieroglyphs correctly, you will discover directions to a secret section of Tut's tomb."

"Oh, my, how very, very exciting," Lucy said. It was like listening to a piece of cardboard talk. "What wonders await us in that secret section?"

"Gold, precious gems—treasure beyond your wildest imagination!" Mr. Myles said. "But first, you have to line up the hieroglyphs on the box correctly. And there are thousands of different combinations."

"If only there was a key," Lucy said.

"Ah, little lady, there is!" Mr. Myles cried happily. "There is a key that shows how to line up the hieroglyphs. And I will show it to you on one of our programs. But I won't tell you which one. You have to keep tuning in! So, we'll see you next week. And if you don't join us—you know what I say? Tut-Tut-Tut!"

37

The audience chuckled and applauded. Mr. Myles made a little bow.

Finally, the red light on the camera went dark.

"And we're off!" the cameraman cried. The entire cast and crew of the show started talking at once, about the power failure, Richard's bizarre accident, and the Secret Map Box.

I slumped against the wall and took a deep breath. Wow, show business sure was a crazy business.

Frank was the only one still working. He wheeled the Secret Map Box past me on its cart. He would lock the box back into its display case and change the combination every night, just to be safe.

As Frank walked by, I noticed someone had taped a sign up next to King Richard's booth. It looked like this:

BEWARE OF THE MUMMY'S CURSE!

It must have been taped up by one of the dancers.

"Is this some kind of joke?" Mr. Myles asked, tearing down the sign as he stormed into the room.

If it was a joke, once again I couldn't find the punch line.

The band practicing on the bus

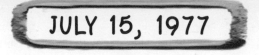

1:50 PM

We're back on the bus, heading up to Cincinnati for another show. The landscape whizzing by is starting to look pretty much the same—billboards, cows, fields . . . and then guess what? Billboards, cows, fields. After a while, everything seems to run together.

It's raining buckets outside, so the windows of the bus are shut, making it like a tropical rain forest in here. The heat and the rocking bus have put most of the kids, Mr. Myles, and even Madame Katerina to sleep.

So things are pretty quiet—except for the six-person band that's practicing the opening number again and again. Listening to a disco band play without electricity is like watching static on TV. It's just a bunch of noise.

Normally, I love music—even though I've got no rhythm. It's the perfect thing for a guy like me who is into mathematical patterns. The bars and notes of a well-structured song shape up into kind of a musical building. In my mind, I can see the logical order of what the next bar or measure should be, like the construction of a skyscraper.

Here's how I see music: Beats are the bricks, measures are the floors, and phrases are big chunks of the building.

The only problem is that every time the musical building starts to go up, Carla, the keyboard player, tears it down. She's a sweet girl my age who has long limbs and a long, sad face. She keeps skipping measures and throwing off the rest of the band. The other musicians laughed about it at first, but after the fourth or fifth time, they stopped laughing.

Carla

"What's wrong with you, Carla?" the lead guitarist asked.

"I don't know," Carla answered with a shrug. "I guess I miss my friends back in Denver."

"Well, you're not going to make new friends playing like that," he told her.

Carla's dark eyes pooled with tears, and she looked down at her hands. "Leave her alone!" I told the guitar player. He looked just as surprised as I did that I had said anything. But I knew what it was like to be homesick and felt sorry for Carla. The guitarist just scoffed at me and said to the rest of the band, "One more time." They started playing again.

R.T., who was sitting a few rows ahead said, "You tell 'em, Enigma!" He suddenly flicked a crumpled ball of paper back at me. I reached up to catch it, and it bounced off my hand, into my glasses, and rolled under my seat. As I

reached for it, I heard Max chuckle from his seat across the aisle and say, "Good catch, four eyes."

But I knew R.T. wasn't being mean. This is part of what we do to keep ourselves from getting too bored. We talk back and forth in coded messages.

I smoothed out the long strip of paper and carefully wound it around my scytale to see what R.T. had to say.

TEC TIP

HOW TO MAKE A SCYTALE

The scytale (which rhymes with Italy) was invented in 404 BCE by Lysander of Sparta, Greece. To make one, wrap a thin strip of paper in a spiral around a rod, such as a pencil or marker. Write your message across the strip. Unwrap the paper. The letters will now look all jumbled up. Send the loose paper to your correspondent, who can then wrap the paper around a rod of equal diameter to the one you used and read your message.

I had just asked R.T. what he had snuck off the breakfast table this morning. His message said:

TO BE OR NOT TO BE THAT IS
AN EGG! ROCKY EATS EM RAW

Sylvester Stallone
played Rocky in
the movie.

He was talking about ROCKY, this movie that just came out. There's this boxer in it who eats raw eggs! R.T. must have nabbed an egg from Madame Katerina's food supplies.

I shook my head, and wound a fresh strip around my scytale. I sent him this message back:

RAW EGG CAUSES SALMONELLA

After reading my coded message, R.T. turned around and looked me, mouthing, "Salmonella?"

I made a face like I was throwing up violently to show him what could happen.

His eyes widened. He turned back to his pad and started writing.

I WILL FRIDGE & EAT LATER!

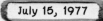

I had run out of strips of paper, so I closed my eyes and listened to the musicians practicing. I could see the musical building almost reach completion—but then Carla would skip the same measure, and the whole thing would come crumbling down. Again and again and again . . .

Backstage in Cincinnati

4:25 PM • CINCINNATI, OHIO

A new city, another museum. We parked our caravan in a side parking lot, watched the guards unload King Tut and his treasures, and got to work setting up our show.

At least the Cincinnati Museum of Historical Antiquities has a much more updated auditorium than the one in New Orleans. There is even a series of pulleys and levers that can raise and lower scenery. In fact, some kind of Roman chariot complete with six ornamental spears was dangling by ropes from the ceiling. The museum must use that for another show.

Our show wouldn't use any of the pulleys—but we did need the electrical system. And that was a dream come true. King Richard, who was still recovering in the hospital down in New Orleans, would have been in heaven!

On the way into the museum, Mr. Myles smacked me on the back. "Kid, if I had my way, I'd keep you as the head lighting technician," he said. "But Richard called the union, and his replacement should be here by show time."

I decided to get things ready for the new guy. I did some simple rearranging of the cables and everything went perfectly during the test run. When the new guy arrived, I went to find a good spot to watch the show. I was nervous for R.T. Madame Katerina had been visited by her Muse again the night before, and the dance had been changed yet again.

47

The dancers had had to learn the new steps in just a few hours.

By the time I found a seat out of the way backstage, I noticed Madame Katerina was standing nearby. She looked incredibly tense, and I thought about moving, but it was too late. It was show time!

I felt a rush when the red light over the camera blinked to life. This time, the local sponsor who introduced the show was an elderly woman. She kept her back incredibly straight, and her icy blue eyes never wavered from the lens of the camera. "Ladies and gentlemen, my name is Asyla Notabe. I am a board member of this museum. It is my great

Asyla Notabe

honor to introduce the TEENS FOR TUT dancers." The woman left the stage, the lights on the dance floor exploded, and the music started playing.

The opening number was going great, and then Carla skipped the same measures in the music. While I found it really jarring, the dancers covered well. They just jumped ahead in the dance until the music and the steps matched up again. And I didn't think the audience noticed.

But Madame Katerina did. I heard her muttering something under her breath, and her hands were clenching her cane so tightly I thought she might snap it in two.

When the red light went out and the show was over, Madame Katerina looked like an angry storm cloud with arms and legs. "My muse is going to be furious!" she whispered.

"Good show, Madame Katerina!" Mr. Myles said, walking up to her with his hands out.

"What do you mean?" she snarled. "That WOMAN and her KEYBOARD!"

"Oh, well. The audience loved the show, that's all that matters," Mr. Myles said and rushed off.

"I'll show her." Madame Katerina stalked toward the band. I had to warn Carla to make herself scarce. I was rushing ahead of the choreographer—when BLAM!

"Coming through!" a stout woman from the audience shouted and actually shoved me aside. As I careened off a few chairs and landed hard on the floor, I noticed the woman had a pearl necklace, pearl earrings, and pearls in the tops of her shoes. And then she was gone.

She must be one unsatisfied customer!

I got to my feet just as Madame Katerina caught up with me. Together, we made our way toward Carla. She saw us coming. Like a panicked animal, she darted the other way, rushing backstage.

"You will HALT!" Madame Katerina commanded, and Carla stopped near the hanging set of the Roman chariot. Her eyes skittered around as if looking for an escape. I thought of the tips my cousin Mal, the outdoor survival specialist, had taught me if I ever encountered a wild animal in the woods.

49

Back away very slowly, he'd said.

And that's exactly what Carla was doing. Inching her way back, as if hoping Madame Katerina would get distracted by other prey.

As Carla retreated, something at her feet caught my eye. She lifted her foot to take another step—

NO!

—and when her foot came back down, her body shot up into the air.

Carla screamed.

A loop of rope had snared her leg when she stepped

Carla was dangling upside down!

into it, and then jerked her about 20 feet up into the air amidst the complicated pulley system. With her long hair flopping over her face, Carla screamed again and again, as she frantically tried to get herself free.

Madame Katerina looked more angry than surprised. "What is the meaning of this? Get down here at once!" The choreographer was acting like Carla had rocketed toward the ceiling on purpose.

"Carla! Don't move!" I called up. But the poor girl was too busy screaming to listen to me.

Carla kept swinging her arms up toward her leg, trying to reach the rope that held her in its grip—and the movement started her whole body swinging. Soon she was ticking back and forth like a giant pendulum on a clock, but this pendulum was speeding up and swinging wider and wider—

"Oh, no!" the lead guitarist shouted. "The spears! She's going to hit the spears!"

And it was true. Carla was getting closer and closer to the tips of the spears from the set. Soon she would smack right into one!

"Carla!" I had to find a way to get her down. "You have to stop yourself from swinging or you'll stab yourself!"

But that just made things worse. Once she saw the spears, she really started to panic, and her body began to swing faster.

Others had gathered around, attracted by Carla's screams. R.T. was one of them, and he held a ladder. "Here," he said and set it underneath the middle of Carla's arc. He climbed to the top and stretched out his hand but couldn't quite reach her as she whizzed back and forth. "Zeke, get

up here and hold me steady, would you?" He called down. I climbed the ladder with shaky legs. I hate heights.

"We have to lower her down," I told R.T.

He gave me a look that said, No kidding, Sherlock. "But how, when there are so many ropes?" he said "I don't want to pull the wrong one! It might swing her closer to the spears!"

"We need help, R.T."

R.T. shook his head. "There's no time," he said, his eyes locking with mine. "You can do this, Enigma."

I looked away from him, frustrated, and tried to make order out of the chaos of the pulley system. Suddenly, I

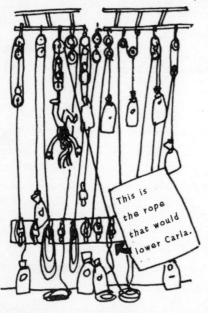

This is the rope that would lower Carla.

felt my mind let go and enter the Code Zone. And everything made perfect sense.

"He's going to jump!" someone screamed from down below. And I realized he meant me.

I stepped off the ladder and grabbed on to the middle rope. There was a click as my weight on the rope caused the pulley to release. As if I were a human sandbag, Carla was lowered to the ground. Max and a few other dancers reached up and gently caught her and lay her on the floor.

"Oh, my leg!" Carla moaned, clutching the leg that had been caught in the snare.

As I watched from above, Lucy's hands flew around the knotted rope. In an instant, she had freed Carla. Without Carla to act as a counterweight, I shot back down toward the ground.

"Enigma!" R.T. was halfway down the ladder and dove off so that his body was between me and the floor. I crashed into him, bounced off, and skidded across the space on my stomach. My head came to rest just inches from the concrete wall.

I had the wind knocked out of me and couldn't move, but I noticed a scrap of paper. It was sitting right in front of my nose and must have been kicked into the corner in all the excitement.

A few hieroglyphs had been drawn above a bunch of jumbled words. It looked like this:

RJ NUXQ KRJ NBXTJ

I reached for the paper. But before my fingers could close around it, Mr. Myles's hand swept down and snatched it up.

"You people have to keep this place clean! Someone could slip on this garbage," he said.

What's he talking about? I wondered as R.T. walked over and gave me a hand to my feet. A piece of paper didn't send Carla flying up into the rafters!

"It's the Curse of King Tut!" the lead guitarist said. And a few of the other kids, who were watching Lucy place a folded jacket under Carla's head, nodded in agreement.

"That curse is nonsense!" Mr. Myles said. "It's an old story I use to fill the seats. Now, someone get me a new keyboard player!"

Lucy scurried over to him and whispered something in his ear. He hesitated for a moment. "Oh, right," he said quietly to her. And then to the rest of us, he bellowed, "And a doctor! Someone call a doctor for this girl! Her leg is broken!"

53

R.T. playing electronic football

R.T. and I were in our room in the trailer. We were ready to move on to the next city, Chicago. But the King Tut exhibition was taking longer than usual to pack up, so we were waiting for all the crates and boxes to be carefully loaded into the special trucks.

With my back against the wall, I sat on one end of my bed. R.T. was on the other end, playing with his electronic football game. It was highly advanced—like the new calculators that could fit into your backpack. The football players were little green blips that blinked on a screen. Almost as good as playing Pong at the arcade.

But this was no time for games.

"Concentrate!" I said and threw a pillow at him.

"What?" he said. "I am! This is how I think!"

"Well, all that beeping and clicking isn't helping me." I stared at the hieroglyphs I had sketched from memory. "How are we going to crack this?"

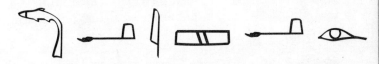

"Crack what?" R.T. said without looking up. "It's from a piece of paper you saw on the dirty floor of the backstage area. It's like Mr. Myles said. The whole thing was an accident. And Carla told me on the way to the hospital that she was glad in a way, because now she'll get to go home."

"There could be a connection between what happened to Carla and Richard," I said. "Do you really think they were both accidents?"

"I don't know." He shrugged. "You've got the brains. I'm dumb as a rock."

R.T. was just finding an excuse to be lazy, but it did get me thinking.

"Dumb as a rock . . . ," I repeated. "Or a stone!"

"Hey!" he shouted. He hadn't expected me to agree with him and fired the pillow back at me. I tried to block it, but it knocked me off the bed. It didn't matter, though, the idea was already lodged in my head.

CHAMPOLLION'S ROSETTA STONE

In 1822, Jean-François Champollion used the Rosetta Stone to translate this text: King Ptolemy, the beloved of Ptah . . . the gods have given him health, victory and power . . . and all other good things.

"If I use the Rosetta Stone," I said still lying on the floor, "I can read what these hieroglyphs say."

"So where are we going to find this stone?" R.T. asked.

"Let's ask our traveling companion."

"Mr. Myles?"

"No," I answered. "King Tut."

R.T. finally looked up from his game.

We rushed into the Cincinnati Museum of Antiquities. This time, though, we went past the auditorium and toward the King Tut exhibition hall.

Normally, there would be a line of thousands of people trying to get a glimpse of Tut. But because the treasures were being packed up for the move to Chicago, the exhibition was closed to visitors for the day.

"How are we going to get in?" R.T. asked.

"I'm not sure," I said. But at the entrance to the hall, I spotted the answer: Frank, the security guard. He was standing next to the Secret Map Box that was still locked up in its case.

Frank

"Hi, Frank," I said. "Mind if we have a quick look in the hall?"

"Hey, boys," Frank said. "Everything is still locked up tight, so I don't think it would be a problem. Just be fast, would you?"

We thanked him and hurried past him into the hall. Glass display cases sat under bright spots of light. The gold objects inside glittered and winked as if they were transmitting a message from the past. There were statues, vases, boxes with jewels, jars that held the mummy's body organs, chests, vessels, thrones, and of course, there was the coffin of King Tut himself.

We were on a mission, but without saying a word, we were both drawn to the mummy of the ancient pharaoh.

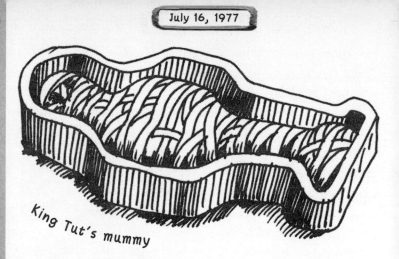

King Tut's mummy

"He looks so together for someone who died more than 3,300 years ago," R.T said.

I explained that when Howard Carter discovered Tut, the king's body was undisturbed. The wrapped mummy had been inside a total of three coffins that had been placed inside each other like Russian dolls. While each coffin contained some gold, the third was made of solid gold—240 pounds of it. That makes it the largest piece of ancient gold craftsmanship ever discovered.

R.T. looked impressed. "Carter was a kind of detective."

"A very patient detective," I said. "It took him ten years to get everything out of King Tut's tomb. He didn't want to miss a single thing." I glanced up and saw Frank pointing at his watch. "Come on, we have to hurry."

We made our way to a display case two rooms away. Inside was an exact copy of the Rosetta Stone. The real stone was in a museum in London, England. But this one would serve our purpose.

I guess I was gazing in awe at the stone, because R.T. asked, "You're jealous of Champollion, aren't you?"

"A little," I said. "I would love the chance to be able to use my code-breaking skills for something so important.

R.T. smiled. "You'll get your chance. I just know it. So what are we looking at?"

"Hieroglyphs were the ancient language of the Egyptians," I said. "They were symbols that could be used to represent a sound and as a word. For example, this symbol," I pointed at the shape of a bird. "It can mean either small or weak . . . or it can stand for the sound 'wr.'"

R.T. nodded. "Got it. But how do you know how to use it?"

"If it was meant to stand for the word, there would be a vertical line beneath it. Like this." I made a slashing motion up and down.

Jewel is a rebus for the throne name of Tut—which translates as "the King is the lord of all creations."

- sun disk at the top = symbol of the sun god, Re

- basket = hieroglyph for all

- scarab beetle = creation, and the three vertical lines underneath make it plural

I did some quick comparisons between the sketch I had made of the hieroglyphs from the scene of Carla's accident to the chart near the stone.

"Hmmm . . . ," I said as it started to come together.

"Okay, Enigma," R.T. said impatiently. "Spill."

"It's not like reading a newspaper. There isn't a direct translation from ancient Egyptian hieroglyphs to English."

"But what do you think it says?"

"CAESAR," I said.

"Caesar?" R.T. asked. "As in Caesar salad?"

"I'm thinking more along the lines of Caesar code."

TEC TIP

THE CAESAR SHIFT CIPHER

This cipher, developed by the Roman emperor it was named after, is easy to create. You simply replace letters in the alphabet with other letters. There are over 400,000,000,000,000,000,000,000,000 combinations. Even if each person in the world were to check one possibility every second, it would take more than 1,000 times the lifetime of a universe to check them all!

R.T. looked at the paper in my hands. "So this is some kind of code."

"Actually, it's a cipher. Codes are when you switch whole words around. Ciphers are trickier because you are switching letters around."

"Okay, that's TMI," he said, meaning Too Much Information. "But we don't have a secret message to decipher!"

"Yes, we do," I told him. "We have—"

"All right, boys!" The sound of Frank's voice interrupted me. He was standing in the doorway of the room. "You're going to have to clear the hall. They're going to start unlocking the display cases, and only authorized personnel are allowed in here at that point."

We thanked Frank and headed out to the parking lot. We found a shady spot near the trailer and sat down on the concrete.

"So what's the message that we have to decode?" R.T. asked impatiently.

"The jumbled words that were written below the hieroglyphs," I told him.

I could still see the message clearly in my mind, one of the advantages of having photographic memory.

I took out my pen and wrote down the words.

RJ NUXQ KRJ NBXTJ

"Okay! That's not helpful," R.T. said.

"But we can make it clear," I said. "We just have to use the frequency chart. It shows the most common letters used in the English language. Then we can make a guess about what letters to swap into the cipher."

Frequency of Letters

LETTER	E	T	A	O	I	N	S	H	R	D	L	U	C	M	F	W	P	G	Y	B	V	K	X	Q	J	Z
PERCENT	10.3	7.8	6.6	6.0	5.8	5.8	5.4	4.8	4.6	3.5	3.2	2.5	2.3	2.0	1.9	1.9	1.5	1.4	1.3	1.2	0.7	0.5	0.1	0.1	0.1	0.1

"E is the letter we use most. So we can start with that," I said. "If you look at the coded message, you'll see J is the most common letter. So J might be the code for E."

"How do you know all this?" R.T. asked. He looked impressed.

I shrugged. "It's called frequency analysis, and it was thought up by a ninth-century scientist known as the philosopher of the Arabs. His name was Abu Yusu Ya'qub ibn Is-haq ibn as-Sabbah ibn 'omran ibn Ismail al-Kindi."

"Say THAT ten times fast," R.T. joked.

But I was on a roll and didn't laugh. "The most common three-letter words are 'the' and 'and.' The most common two letter pairs are 'ss,' 'ee,' 'tt,' 'ff,' 'll,' 'mm,' and 'oo.'"

R.T. shook his head. "But there aren't any letter pairs. There is a three-letter word, though."

"Let's try 'the' in its place."

If 'the' was right, that would mean that the H, which had been substituted for the R in the three-letter word, would also take the place of the R at the beginning of the message, and the E for the J would swap in for the other two Js as well.

Soon the message looked like this:

HE NUXQ THE NBXTE

"It says 'He BLANK the BLANK.'"

"Who's he?" R.T. asked. "And what did he do?"

"That's what I'm trying to figure out. Give me a second." I stared at the page and let myself go into the Code Zone.

After a few moments, I cried, "I think I have it!" I wrote down the words that filled my mind.

"Let me see." R.T. took the page from my hands and read it out loud. 'He paid the price.' What does that mean?"

"It could be talking about Richard or Carla."

"But Carla's a she not a he. And you and I saw Richard's accident. You were the last person to touch the sand. Do you have something you want to confess?" he asked with a smile.

"If only Lucy hadn't untied the knot from that rope, we might have been able to tell if someone had tied it on purpose."

"And you would still be swinging from the rafters. Those hieroglyphs could have come from anywhere, Zeke. We're traveling with a bunch of old Egyptian stuff. Maybe someone got Tut to sign his autograph or something. It's probably just a wild coincidence."

I looked glumly down at the paper. It had seemed so clear a moment ago, but now I didn't know. "That would make as much sense as this, I guess."

Madame Katerina changed the dance again!

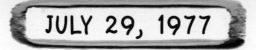

8:20 AM • CHICAGO, ILLINOIS

Last night, we pulled into the Windy City, and our caravan parked in the raised parking lot behind the Museum of Ancient Art. Everyone's a little frayed around the edges. Which isn't good. Not only will this be our last show but the biggest—the Secret Map Box will be unlocked at the end!

The stage here is the best yet. There is an actual control room up near the ceiling behind the audience. Mr. Myles will be able to sit up there and boss people around.

In fact, he shouted from the control room's window for me to sweep up the stage before the dancers started rehearsal. Madame Katerina had already gathered the dancers on stage as I swept around them. She was giving them a pre-rehearsal pep talk, but it quickly went sour.

"My Muse visited again last night," Madame Katerina told them.

The dancers groaned, and one kid even kneeled down and started pounding the floor in frustration.

"Stop whining!" she shouted, slamming her ballet stick down. And the complaining instantly stopped. "Final show is not for five days. We have plenty of time to get right!"

This time, she explained, the lead dancer must make a massive leap almost all the way across the dance floor without touching the ground. While he's doing that, the chorus had to mirror this move with shorter—but still near-impossible—leaps.

"That's crazy!" the dancers shouted, Max the loudest.

But Madame Katerina didn't want to hear it. "You will do the dance exactly as instructed. Now I must speak to Mr. Myles regarding business matter. YOU will rehearse new moves."

Madame Katerina swept off the stage with the tails of her headscarf flapping behind her. While I continued to sweep, the dancers started flinging their bodies across the stage, trying to follow her choreography. They looked like a bunch of crazed puppets that had just had their strings cut. It was hard to watch, and I put my head in my hands.

"You think it's easy?"

I looked up startled. Max was standing in front of me. "Let's see you give it a try."

I glanced at R.T. He just grinned and shrugged. He wasn't going to help me—he had always wanted to get me to try a dance move or two, and now was my chance.

"That's what I thought," Max said, taking my silence as a refusal to dance.

Something about the way Max turned away, as if I wasn't really worth his time, changed my mind.

"All right," I said. I set down the broom and stepped into the rehearsal area.

Surprised, Max said, "Okay, good. Come over here. The dance steps go 1, 2, 3 . . . and then 4."

Max made the leap but stumbled on the landing and fell to his hands and knees.

"Exactly. Except you're not supposed to fall down," R.T. said with a small smile.

"No problem," I said. This is it, I thought. This is the moment that I change my life around. I'm not just some brainiac, I'm a disco-dancing boogie machine.

1, 2, 3 . . .

I could see myself in my mind's eye flying across the space, and the entire room awestruck and cheering my dancing abilities. But in reality, my feet skittered to halt like a plane suddenly putting on the brakes as it was heading down the runway.

"That's all right, Enigma," R.T. said, putting a hand on my shoulder. "It's a tough move."

"Time to go back to the farm," Max sneered.

R.T. didn't say anything, but the smile on his face froze. And without even looking at Max, he walked to the far end of the rehearsal space.

Max must have thought he was fleeing, because he laughed nastily. "That's right, go on back to your cows and your—"

R.T. spun around and suddenly, he was dancing. He went through the steps. 1, 2, 3—he was flying through the air—and BLAM! He landed on his feet.

Only then did R.T. look at Max. "I'm sorry, did you say something?"

R.T. could do Max's leap.

Max was speechless for a second and then said, "Huh. Nice job."

67

Madame Katerina and
Mr. Myles were arguing.

The dancers went back to rehearsing, and I went back to pushing my broom. I was under the control room when I heard the voices of Madame Katerina and Mr. Myles. From this angle, I couldn't see them, but it was clear they were having a heated argument.

"You cannot expect me to work with this amateur any longer," she was saying. "I want him this instant fired!"

"Why?" Mr. Myles said. "Even if Max only does half the leap, it still looks good. Besides, we signed a contract with the kid, and his parents could sue us. I'm not firing him."

A moment passed, and I could almost see Madame Katerina trying to control her rage. She nodded and said, "You're right, of course, Mr. Myles. I am feeling the stress of the situation."

There was suddenly a huge crash from the stage. I looked up in time to see one of the dancers trip and bounce off a nearby wall.

I realized Madame Katerina wasn't the only one feeling the stress.

The next day, I woke up from a nightmare with a code in my head. I'd been reading Sir Arthur Conan Doyle's book THE ADVENTURES OF THE DANCING MEN, where he uses stick figures in different poses to represent letters of the alphabet. Ever since I started reading the Sherlock Holmes book, which Richard had lent me, I'd been dreaming about

Holmes's mortal enemy—Moriarty—only in my dreams, the evil villain never had a face.

With the code from my dream fresh in my mind, I thought Richard would get a kick out of it. He was still in the New Orleans hospital. And he might be lonely.

Careful not to wake up R.T., I climbed out of bed and began writing down the code that was in my head. A code doesn't have to use just letters or symbols, it can use pictures or planets—or even a pony named Teddy.

At the bottom of the code, I added a quick P.S. asking Richard if he had seen anything strange before or after his accident.

I stuck the code in an envelope and addressed it to King Richard at the New Orleans hospital. This should help keep him busy while he recovers, I thought.

I headed out of the trailer and left the parking lot in search of a mailbox. A fancy hotel stood across the street from the museum, and I spotted a mailbox there.

I was dropping the letter in the mailbox when . . .

"Hello, Zeke."

That voice!

Feeling my heart leap, I turned—and came face to face with Judge Pinkerton!

"Judge!" I blurted and threw myself into her open arms. I hadn't realized how homesick I'd been until this very second.

Judge's real name is Justine Pinkerton, and she's an old family friend.

She used to be a big judge in San Francisco, but even before then, my family always called her

THE FIRST PRIVATE EYE

Born in 1819, Allan Pinkerton was America's first private investigator and started the Pinkerton National Detective Agency. The company's motto was "We never sleep" and its logo was an unblinking eye—which led to the term "private eye." During his life, Pinkerton foiled an attempt to assassinate President Lincoln, tracked down outlaws such as Jesse James, and invented the mug shot, which was used on reward posters in the Wild West.

Judge is a Pinkerton!

Judge. I think it all started with my Great-Great-Grandma Fitz and a train. Judge recently left San Francisco and started her own security and bodyguard agency that she runs out of Washington State.

I let go of Judge and took a step backward. "Are you okay?" she asked, her sharp blue eyes examining me.

"I'm fine," I smiled. "I'm just glad to see you."

Mrs. Craffin

She nodded, satisfied for now. "Zeke," Judge said, pointing to an old woman next to her. "I'd like you to meet my friend Alexandra Craffin."

Aha! So this was the woman who had the key to the Secret Map Box! I couldn't wait to talk to her!

The woman waved her ivory-handled cane at me like an accusing finger. "It's hot. Why is Chicago called the Windy City? There is no wind! There's not even a breeze!" She spoke with such fury that I really didn't know how to reply.

"Yes, I, uh . . . ," I stammered.

Judge rescued me by turning to a kid about twice my size who looked to be about sixteen. He was wearing a white polyester suit with an open-collared silk shirt.

"And this is her nephew, James," Judge said.

I stuck out my hand to shake, but James ducked away as if I was swinging a hammer. "The hair!" he cried. "Don't touch the hair!"

"I wasn't going to," I mumbled. Who on earth was Judge traveling with?

James

71

He eyed me suspiciously and then said, "Call me John."

And then I got it. The clothes, the name, the fussing about the hair. He was trying to be like John Travolta, the disco-dancing superstar in SATURDAY NIGHT FEVER.

A hand reached up to swat "John's" head. "Step aside, you big lug!"

"The hair!" James cried. But he moved and when he did, I could see the source of the swatting. It was an incredibly pretty girl, about fifteen years old.

Nora

"Ah." Judge seemed relieved to focus on the girl for a moment. Her olive skin looked flawless, and her jet-black hair was worn loose and long, framing her head in a soft dark halo. "And this is Mrs. Craffin's niece, Nora."

"Nice to meet you," I said and shook her hand. I could feel my face start burning instantly. Trying to cover, I turned back to Judge. "What are you doing here?"

"We're checking into this hotel." She gestured toward a large pile of luggage directly behind her. "A taxi just dropped us off from the airport. I'm here with Mrs. Craffin."

The old woman waved her cane again. "She is guarding me and my family. We have been acquainted for years."

"That's right," Judge said. "In fact, we were born the same year: 1897."

It was hard to believe
that they were the same age.
Mrs. Craffin looked even older
than eighty, as if some unseen
weight were slowly bending
her body. But Judge looked as
glamorous as ever. Her back
was straight, and she was nearly
6 feet tall in her purple heels.

Judge looks great for an eighty-year-old!

"How is your brother?"
she asked.

"Chitchat?" wheezed
Mrs. Craffin at Judge. "You're
working for me."

Judge's eyes grew cool as she turned them on the
other woman. "That will do, Alex. I am here as a favor to
you. You won't let anyone else watch out for you, and I'm
not sure you could pay them enough to do it anyway."

Mrs. Craffin was looking around fearfully. "Shhh . . . he
has ears everywhere."

I raised an eyebrow at Judge, who rolled her eyes.

"It's been a long trip," Judge said. "Zeke, we'll catch
up later. I want to get Mrs. Craffin settled in her room and
do a quick check of the area."

"Okay, Judge," I said. "We're in a trailer parked behind
the museum."

Judge nodded with a smile. "Your parents told me. I'll
find you."

"Bring in the bags. I don't want to tip any bellboys,"
Mrs. Craffin told James and Nora as Judge led her into
the hotel.

"This heat is killing my hair," James said and darted quickly after them into the cool air of the lobby.

That left poor Nora alone, struggling with all the bags. Suddenly, one of the bags slipped from her hands and tumbled back onto the sidewalk.

I rushed over to her. "Here. Let me help you."

"Thanks," she said.

We managed to strap several pieces of luggage over our shoulders and hold the rest by the handles. The bags were under control. But I made no move to enter the hotel. I wanted to talk more with this girl—and we just stood on the blazing-hot sidewalk. "Do you travel with your aunt all the time?" I finally asked.

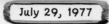

"This isn't a vacation for me," Nora said. "I'm working for her during the summer holiday. I'm kind of her secretary. I type up her notes. At least it gives me a chance to check out the King Tut exhibit close up."

"Are you an Egyptologist?" I asked.

"It runs in my family," she said and then, her eyes met mine. "Kind of the way detective skills run in yours."

"How do you know that?"

"I read THE INSPECTOR, and Ms. Pinkerton talks about your family all the time. She's very proud of you," Nora said. "And, of course, I'm interested in the work she does. I would love to talk to you more about it. Maybe over a soda or something?"

I hoped my face hadn't turned bright red and that I didn't say, "Yes!" too fast.

Judge and R.T. by the turtle po in the zoo

5:00 PM

R.T., Judge, and I were walking through the Chicago Zoo. Judge had told us she wanted to talk someplace where we wouldn't be disturbed.

The sun was pounding down on us, and I felt sweat rolling down my back. But Judge, as always, looked fresh and energetic in her purple slacks and white blouse.

R.T. and I had had a chance to catch up with her. Now she was telling us about Mrs. Craffin as the three of us strolled by the turtle pond. "Mrs. Craffin wasn't always like she is today. We spent a year in boarding school together, and we would get each other laughing so hard." Judge smiled at the memory and then shook her head sadly. "But that was a long time ago. She has a kind heart, it's just been buried by years of living in fear. And since her husband died last year, I'm afraid she's grown even colder."

"Why is Mrs. Craffin so afraid?" I asked.

Judge said, "She received two disturbing notes."

"Did they threaten her?" R.T. asked.

She shook her head. "No, they never hinted at any violence. But they did demand that Mrs. Craffin return her ankh necklace to its rightful owner."

I asked, "How did she get an ankh necklace to begin with?"

The ankh necklace

"It's a pretty amazing story," Judge said, and we paused near the monkey house so she could have our full attention. "On November 4, 1922, a water boy with Carter's archaeological team dug a hole for his water jar and found the first step that led to King Tut's tomb. The tomb was pretty much untouched by grave robbers. It was like opening a doorway into the past, with treasures people normally only dream about."

"I still don't see the connection between the Craffins and the tomb," R.T. said.

"Mrs. Craffin's husband was the water boy," Judge said. "He felt that since he had been the one to find the entrance to the tomb, he deserved at least a small token for himself."

"So he took it," I guessed.

Judge nodded. "He was young and foolish, and secretly took an ankh necklace from the tomb. Since that time, his family has fallen prey to some extremely bad luck. Some might even call it the Craffin Curse, a kind of extension of the Curse of the Mummy. There have been several accidents

VALLEY OF THE KINGS

On the west bank of the Nile River, about 416 miles south of Cairo, lay two desert canyons covering half a square mile. Home to at least 62 tombs of Egyptian pharaohs and nobles, including King Tut's, the area is called the Valley of the Kings. King Tut took the throne around 1332 BCE, when he was about eight or nine. Ten years later, he died. Some think he might have been murdered.

over the years. Still, Mr. Craffin refused to give up the necklace. And after his death, my friend continued to hold onto it. She felt like her family had paid a huge price for it with their suffering. But then she received the notes and decided enough was enough."

"That's why she's going to give the ankh necklace back on the TEENS FOR TUT show?" R.T. asked.

"Yes," Judge said. "She asked me to watch out for her until she hands over the ankh necklace."

"So what's so important about this necklace?" I asked.
Judge said, "That's what you discovered."

I was so caught up in the flow of the story that her words caught me off guard. I looked at Judge, confused. "That's what WHO discovered?"

She never took her eyes off mine. "The person who has been following us and listening in on our conversation." With that, she turned and spoke to someone who was standing in the shadows of a few nearby trees.

It was Nora!

79

She took a few quick steps toward us, looking embarrassed. "I'm sorry, I wasn't trying to eavesdrop. I wanted to give you this message from my aunt." Nora handed Judge a slip of paper. "It's nothing urgent."

"Do you want to finish the story, Nora?" Judge asked.

Nora nodded. "Okay. I came into the picture after my uncle died. I was helping to clean up his office and donate some of his studies to different universities. When I found the ankh, I knew it could be the key to unlocking the five layers of the Secret Map Box. It might be the key that could reveal the map and lead archaeologists to one of the most important discoveries from the ancient world."

Nora found the necklace on her uncle's desk.

"Where did you find it in his office?" R.T. asked. "Was it hidden?"

"It was in an envelope with the words 'Egyptian Uni.' I think my uncle was going to send the ankh back where it belonged, to the Egyptian University, to the people of Egypt."

"But your aunt disagreed?" I asked.

Nora's lips tightened. "The address wasn't complete, so she believed what she wanted to believe."

Judge hesitated. She looked at me and then at Nora. I could tell there was more she wanted to say but not in front of Nora. R.T. picked up on it, too.

He turned to Nora. "Hey, want to see the monkey house? You can see why I feel right at home there."

She looked at me and then at him. She wasn't dumb, she knew we what we were trying to do. "Sure . . ."

I watched the two of them walk away and felt a sharp pang of jealousy, but I tried to push it aside. Judge obviously had something important to discuss with me. Plus, I wanted to tell her about the "accidents" that had been occurring lately.

"What is it, Judge?"

"I want to show you something. You are so good at seeing patterns, Zeke. What can you see on these notes? Do they trigger anything in the Code Zone?" Judge removed two pieces of paper sealed in plastic from her purse and handed them to me.

"What are these?" I asked.

"These are the two messages Mrs. Craffin received." Here's what they said:

DO WHAT IS RIGHT.
RETURN THE ANKH.

SEND THE ANKH HOME.
NOW IS THE TIME.

"Fingerprints?" I asked.

"No," Judge said. "Only Mrs. Craffin's."

"Fibers?"

"Nothing that we can trace."

"How about the ink?"

"No. These are typewritten notes that could have been composed on any one of the millions of typewriters out there. So it would be nearly impossible to find the one it came from." She tapped the notes thoughtfully. "You're the code expert. I need to know if you see any patterns. Any hidden messages that I might be missing."

"No," I said, and Judge sighed in relief. But I continued, "Except there is one thing . . ." I asked Judge if she had a magnifying glass in her purse, and she handed one over.

Whenever it was used, the A was slightly chipped.

I took a closer look at one of the notes. "Check out the A."

"The A?"

"Yes. It's slightly chipped. You find the typewriter that makes an A like that and you are one step closer to finding the person who used it to type these notes."

"Bully for you, Zeke!" Judge had taken the magnifying glass and was examining the A. "Still, I think the notes are a hoax. There aren't any threats in them."

I opened my mouth to tell her about other possible threats. But Judge said something that kept my lips sealed. "Otherwise," she told me, "I would send you and your brother home right now."

I'm glad Judge was too busy examining the notes to notice the look on my face. Suddenly, I was torn. I wanted to tell her my suspicions about the strange "accidents" that had been occurring with the TEENS FOR TUT group. But Judge would call our parents and send us back to Nebraska before R.T. had the chance to be in the big show. I was doing it for R.T., I told myself, but I wasn't being completely honest. There was another reason.

"Nora!" Judge called, as if reading my mind. If we got sent home, I wouldn't be able to hang out with Nora. "Why don't you have Zeke show you the secret language of the iguanas? It's really fascinating."

I gave Judge a grin. She's the best.

R.T. and Max trying to outdo each other

5:10 PM

It had been a while since the dancers
had rehearsed the Dancing Egyptian Queen number—which
involved disco roller-skating. Madame Katerina said, "You
children are getting lazy. Rehearse the number while I
consult with my Muse."

I helped get the dancers into their costumes and
stuck around to watch them run through the number twice.
That's when R.T. and Max started daring each other to do
little stunts.

It started when R.T. leaped over a mop handle that had
fallen on the floor. Max then jumped over the mop from
one end to the other. Then they put the mop up on two
chairs—and jumped over that.

"Face!" they kept shouting at each other, which is
what everyone said when they felt like they were outdoing
someone.

Soon they ran out of challenges inside, and they headed
out to the parking lot and continued with their little game,
this time on skates. I got bored watching them and went
back inside to something more exciting—the craft services
table. I wasn't the only one with that idea—the tall chorus
girl and her friend were there.

"What is THIS?" The tall chorus girl whined. "There's a
big loaf of moldy bread out here!"

Yuck, I thought. It wasn't like Madame Katerina to allow
something like that on her food tables.

Oh, well, I thought, and had just popped two pizza rolls

85

into my mouth when I heard a voice that sounded like soft music to me.

"Zeke."

I turned and spotted Nora sitting with her brother, James, against the wall. She was putting on her skates, and he was just staring at his. Nora waved me over, and when I got there, she looked up at me from her seat on the floor and said, "Hi! How are you?"

"Hine!" I said. Somehow my brain had combined "hi" with "fine." And to make things worse, I had forgotten about my mouthful of pizza rolls, and small crumbs went flying.

Nora acted like she didn't notice, and I swallowed quickly, trying to think of what R.T. would say in a situation like this.

"James and I—" Nora broke off when her brother nudged her. She started over. "JOHN and I came over with our aunt and Ms. Pinkerton to check out the stage. The two of us were going to skate outside in the parking lot, but he changed his mind."

"Too windy out there today," James explained. "Not good for the hair."

"You want to use his skates?" Nora asked me. "John won't mind, will you John?"

James didn't answer, but left his skates and huffed off.

I still had not said one word that made

sense. Nora patted the spot next to her. "Here. Take a seat and put them on. Let's give them a try."

I sat down next to her and tied the skates on. Then we headed outside to join the others. The raised parking lot where our caravan was parked had been blocked off to other traffic—and the long three-story ramp that led down to the street had been closed with orange construction cones. The lot was the perfect spot for roller-skating— that is, it would have been if I knew how to skate.

NORA CAN REALLY SKATE!

But as I discovered after about two seconds, Nora was really good.

I didn't know what to say as I stumbled along next to her. Ask her about herself. Keep her talking and you won't have a chance to put your foot in your mouth. "You're a great skater. What else do you like to do?"

"Well, I'm an amateur Egyptologist—and that's led me to a little detective work. Nothing like your family, but I helped a local art dealer figure out he was about to buy a fraud. There's this husband and wife team of archaeologists called the Vettles."

"Really?"

She nodded. "That's why I'm so interested in the work your friend Justine Pinkerton does. Are there any new leads with the notes that my aunt received?"

I wanted to tell Nora whatever she wanted to know. But detectives didn't talk about each other's work while they were on a job.

"You should probably ask Judge about that. It's her case," I said. Nora looked disappointed, and there was an awkward silence. I decided to change the subject. "So . . . everything is leading up to two days from now. Your aunt will make an appearance after the dance and return the ankh?"

"That's the plan. I think my aunt would have given the ankh to the exhibition two weeks ago, but your producer convinced her to wait until tomorrow so he could hype the big event." She slowed down and looked at me. "Well, it keeps us around for a little while longer."

I was just about to say that I was glad when something caught my eye—

A small piece of paper was fluttering on the back of Max's right skate. It flapped free and was caught in the breeze. I snatched it out of the air without thinking and looked at it.

"That kid shouldn't litter," Nora said.

But I didn't say anything. I was too stunned. On the paper was a series of hieroglyphs.

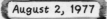

The last time I had found a hieroglyph, there had just been an accident.

Was something bad about to happen?

Just to be safe, I called out, "Hey, Max, you might want to—"

Max turned his head toward me and opened his mouth to say something. At that very moment, the back two wheels of his right skate snapped off. The wheels bounced and skittered off to the side of the parking lot.

Suddenly, Max's face was a mask of confusion and panic. It might have been comic if it wasn't potentially deadly.

He teetered on the edge of the ramp and then he was rushing down it.

Without thinking, I headed after him. I found myself able to skate better than I thought.

Max's weight was balanced on his left skate. I would have just sat down on my backside. But by then, Max was going way too fast. He was careening down the ramp, his arms pinwheeling as he tried to keep his balance.

At the bottom of the ramp, he shot across a small back street and rammed full speed into the curb. He shot into the air and rolled through the open gate of a chain-link fence that surrounded a small auto parts lot.

The sound of savage barking exploded and echoed up the ramp of the parking lot. By the time, Nora, R.T., and I got to the bottom, it was clear where the barks were coming from. Two rottweilers had been chained up inside the fence. Why someone needed them to protect rusted-out cars and old tires was beyond me—but right now, that didn't seem to matter.

Max looked terrified!

The dogs were snapping at the air, straining to reach Max, who lay still between them. The wheels of his intact skate were still spinning.

Without thinking, I headed toward the gate. But both R.T. and Nora pulled me back.

"No," R.T. said. "You can't go in there. Those dogs will tear you to shreds."

"But we have to get Max out of there," I said.

"Right now, he's lying in the exact spot where the dogs can't reach," Nora said.

I had a plan. I sat down and took off my skates so I could move more easily.

I told R.T. to go to one side of the fence and Nora to the other. If they could pull the dogs' attention over to them, I might be able to sneak through the gate and save Max.

"I'll do it," R.T. said.

"No," I said. "You'll be able to move faster and distract the dogs better on skates. I'll just fall down."

They agreed and went to their places. They started shouting crazily at the dogs, waving their arms and skating in quick short circles. I noticed Nora got a little too close at one point and nearly lost a hand to one of the dog's snapping jaws.

The dogs were distracted, which gave me a chance to run and help Max up. He leaned against my shoulder, and we hurried back toward the gate.

Just as we were about to slip free, a rottweiler latched onto Max's right skate. I leaned down and plucked the lace free. It slid off his foot, and the dog was distracted for a moment. And then it ripped the skate to shreds.

Max and I fell into a heap, and I clenched up, waiting for the dog's teeth to clamp down on me.

But when I looked around, I saw that we had fallen out of the gate. We were safe!

Nora and R.T. skated over to us.

"Wow," Nora said. "That was one of the bravest things I've ever seen."

R.T. just grinned at me.

Together, the three of us helped Max back to the museum.

6:50 PM

About twenty minutes after Max's accident, Judge was in our room. R.T. and I sat on the lower bunk. There was no room for a chair, so Judge leaned against the wall next to the poster of CHARLIE'S ANGELS star Farrah Fawcett that R.T. had taped up.

"I heard about what happened," she said. "Are you two okay?"

R.T. said, "We're okay. Mr. Myles probably picked up those skates from Busted Wheels R Us."

"Zeke?" she said, looking me in the eyes. "Are you fine? Do I have to call your parents?"

I was torn. I thought of the paper with the hieroglyphs I had discovered in the parking lot. But I didn't mention it. Instead, I said, "No, Judge, we're okay."

Judge kept her eyes on me a moment longer. I could tell she wasn't really sure whether to believe me. But she finally nodded.

"All right then, I'm glad to hear it," Judge said. "I'd better get back to Mrs. Craffin." She paused and added, "Oh, and congratulations, R.T., Mr. Myles told me you're the new lead dancer since Max sprained his ankle."

"Thanks," R.T. said. "Kind of a crummy way to get the job, but I'm excited."

"You should be," Judge said, opening the door. "Watch out for yourselves."

"Why should we when you're doing it for us?" R.T. said with a charming smile.

93

Judge chuckled and shook her head as she left our room. After she was gone, I went back to what I'd been doing when she came into the room five minutes earlier. I examined the hieroglyphs that had flown off the back of Max's skate.

"Why didn't you tell Judge about that clue?" R.T. asked.

"What do you mean?" I asked as innocently as I could.

"Ha!" he replied.

"Okay," I said, coming clean. "I didn't want to tell her about it—yet."

"Why?" he asked, and then his eyes lit up with understanding. "Oh, I know why. Does this have anything to do with a certain person named Nora? That if we tell Judge, she'll send you home and you won't have a chance to go for long walks with your—"

"Stop! I'm warning you!"

"—with your girlfriend?"

I tried tackling him, but he sidestepped out of the way, and I landed hard on the bed. "Well, what about you? You've just been made lead dancer. Do you want to go back home now?"

That got to him. "All right," he said. "But we'll tell her after the show. Agreed?"

"Agreed," I said. "Now let me see if I can make sense of these hieroglyphs."

He sat on the bed next to me as I worked. After ten more minutes, I finally cracked it. The hieroglyphs said:

HISTAIAEUS

TEC TIP

SLOW DELIVERY

If you're not in a hurry and have someone you can order around, you might send secret messages the way Histiaieus did. This Greek ruler would shave a servant's head, write a message on the bare skin, then wait for the hair to grow back. Then he'd send the servant to the recipient, who would shave the servant's head and read the message.

R.T. and I talked about what the clue might mean.

"What about James?" R.T. said. "He's always talking about his hair. He could be the bad guy. Or working with them. He could have a secret message on his head right now!"

"Come on!" I said. "You don't think that kid is the villain!"

"Who knows?" R.T. said with a mischievous gleam in his eyes. "But it could be fun to find out."

95

Nora let me know Jan was in his bedroo

AUGUST 3, 1977

12:30 PM

Nora opened the door to the suite she was staying in with her brother and aunt. Overlooking Lake Michigan, it had a large living room, which was shared by the three bedrooms. The smell of Mrs. Craffin's lavender perfume hung in the air as Nora let me in. But I knew that she was with Judge at lunch.

Nora pointed to a closed bedroom door and mouthed, "James is in there!"

Out loud, Nora said, "Zeke! What's up?"

"Have you heard the news?" I asked her, loud enough for James to hear. This was all part of the setup we had discussed and scripted earlier.

"No, what news is that?" Nora asked, leading me into the living room.

"John Travolta is going to star in the movie version of Pet Rock," I told her.

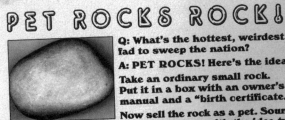

PET ROCKS ROCK!

Q: What's the hottest, weirdest fad to sweep the nation?

A: PET ROCKS! Here's the idea: Take an ordinary small rock. Put it in a box with an owner's manual and a "birth certificate."

Now sell the rock as a pet. Sound silly? Not to Gary Dahl, who came up with the idea two years ago. Since then, he's sold more than five million Pet Rocks! Everybody wants one—maybe because they never beg at dinner or have to be house trained.

"Really?" Nora said. "How exciting!"

"I ran out and bought this electric razor, Nora. It's the same kind John Travolta used to shave his head for the part He now looks like a Pet Rock."

This was ridiculous. My dad helped people detect cons and scams all the time, but no one would ever fall for this.

R.T. pretending to be bald

That's when R.T. walked in wearing a skullcap from the makeup department. From a distance, I guessed someone might think he looked bald, but I could see where a few strands of hair had escaped the plastic.

"Do you like it?" R.T. asked.

"Sweet!" I said, thinking I must have sounded as flat as Lucy.

"You look awesome, R.T.!" Nora cried. She was definitely a better actor.

Nora had agreed to help us carry out our plan. She said she was tired of constantly hearing about her brother's hair and how no one should touch it. Plus, she had a condition: If she helped us, I had to agree to talk to her more about the work Judge does.

There was the click of a door opening across the room, and we all turned. James was now standing in the doorway to his bedroom.

He looked at us suspiciously. "I'm president of the San Francisco John Travolta Fan Club. I would've heard about this." He didn't bother acting as if he hadn't been eavesdropping.

R.T. smiled at him. "We're in show business, so we get the inside scoop first."

I waited for James to shout, "No way!" or "I can tell you're wearing a fake skullcap—it's so obvious." But instead, he just nodded. He was satisfied by R.T.'s lame explanation. James headed toward the electric razor.

This was supposed to be fun—but it was too easy and too mean. Nora must have been thinking the same thing because she was looking down guiltily.

"Wait!" I said, and stood between John and the razor. "You can't use that."

"Why not?"

"Because . . . because it's broken."

"You just don't want to share," James whined and stormed back into his bedroom, slamming the door behind him.

"Well, that was a waste of time," R.T. said, plopping down in an easy chair. "Especially when you decided to pull the plug on our plan without even asking me."

"What plan? That was like a sketch from SATURDAY NIGHT LIVE," I said. "He's too easy to trick. Let's turn back to the case. We need to think of other things that you might need to shave. Things that can be written on and then covered up, like a bald head that is covered with hair."

99

"What about a shaved cat?" R.T. suggested.

"Or farmland that's covered in crops. When they harvest the crops, you could read the message," Nora said.

"From a plane?" R.T. said doubtfully.

I started to come to Nora's rescue, but I broke off when James's door opened again and he came out. Nora gasped. In a low voice, R.T. said, "Dude . . ." But I was stunned speechless.

James's head was perfectly bald.

"What did you do?" I finally managed to ask.

"I have a razor in there, you know, for when I need to start shaving," James said, as his eyes took in R.T.'s full head of hair. "Hey, what happened?"

I walked slowly over to James. I didn't know what to say.

James shaved his head!

"What do you see, Enigma?" R.T. asked.

I looked at James's bald head, but we already knew the answer. "There's no message. There's nothing." I said.

And that's what I felt like after what had just happened. In fact, I felt like less than nothing.

A few minutes later, we were sitting in the living room. We had just told James the truth. He sat on one of the sofas with his head in his hands. "You mean there is no PET ROCK: THE MOVIE?"

"No," I told him.

"And you *thought* I had some secret message on my head?" he moaned.

"Yes, I guess," I said, then decided to come completely clean. "I mean, no, not really."

Tears were welling up in his eyes. "So it was just for fun that you had me shave my head!"

"We tried to stop you!" Nora said.

"You tricked me." James looked down, and tears streamed down his cheeks.

"He's right. I feel like we just used our powers for evil," R.T. said under his breath.

"Give me a second alone with him?" Nora said to us.

R.T. wandered over to the window, and I walked over to the desk Nora had taken over and set up as her portable traveling office.

Just then, the door opened. Judge came in first, I guess to make sure the room was safe. She eyed the situation quickly and turned. "Alex, let's go downstairs and have a cup of coffee."

But it was too late. Mrs. Craffin had pushed her way into the room, her cane waving wildly in the air. Her eyes widened in terror when she saw James. "The curse! The curse has made you bald!"

"No," Judge said, trying to calm her. "I'm sure there's an explanation for this. Probably not a very good one, but some explanation."

But Mrs. Craffin was staggering, as if she was having some kind of attack.

Nora rushed to her. Everyone was shouting and rushing about.

DING!

For some reason that simple sound caused everyone to freeze in their positions. For a moment, they all looked like a painting on the wall of an ancient tomb.

"What is that sound?" Mrs. Craffin asked.

"Why don't you tell her?" I said. I was standing over the typewriter, one finger over the A key.

Mrs. Craffin looked at me like I was nuts. "Who on Earth are you talking to?"

"The person who sent you those notes," I told her.

All eyes went to James, but it was Nora who spoke.

"How do you know I did it?" Her pretty face was transformed by a storm of panic. She had the look of a trapped animal. "A lot of people have typewriters."

I hit the key again and again. Each time I did so, I could see Nora cringe.

"The A made by this typewriter is chipped," I said.

Finally, Nora spoke. "You're right," she said.

Mrs. Craffin sank into a chair, while Judge took a bottle of water from the room's mini fridge and handed it to her. Mrs. Craffin took a long drink. "So it's not a curse . . ."

"No, Auntie. I'm sorry."
Nora turned to me. "When I found the necklace among Uncle's things, I knew immediately that it was the missing ankh. I took it to my aunt right away. But she refused to give it back. It was wrong for my family to keep the ankh any longer."

"It was ours," Mrs. Craffin said stubbornly.

"It belongs to King Tut and the Egyptian people," Nora said. "I sent her the notes. I'm sorry I lied to you, Zeke."

I looked at her and suddenly, my face felt hot again. But this time from anger. "You were just using me to find out about Judge's investigation. You wanted to see if she suspected you. That's why you were so nice to me."

"No!" Nora cried.

"Tell the truth," I said.

"At first, that might have been the reason. But I like you, Zeke. I like spending time with you," Nora said, placing a hand on my shoulder. "You have to believe me."

But I didn't know what to believe. I shook off her hand and looked down.

"If there is no curse and Nora sent the notes . . ." Mrs. Craffin's bony fingers closed around the ankh necklace. "Then I could keep the necklace."

103

"You're right about that, Alex," Judge told her. "You could hold onto the necklace. But I wouldn't say that there's no curse."

"Look what's it done to your family," I said. And Mrs. Craffin's watery eyes moved from her nephew with his shaved head to her niece who stood in the corner with tears rolling down her face.

"Of course. You're right," Mrs. Craffin said. "There was a curse. But I can see now it was of our own making. It's time for me to stop living for a 3,000-year-old object and live in the present."

"Bully for you, my friend," Judge said quietly and stepped back. Mrs. Craffin held out her hands. James came over first and took one. Nora hesitated until her aunt reached out for her again. "Nora, please."

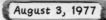

The girl went to her. "I'm so sorry, Auntie."

"No," Mrs. Craffin soothed. "I'm the one who needs to apologize. Let's break this curse, once and for all. You two need to go home and get on with your lives. I'm sending you back to San Francisco this evening. I'll stay here and finish up this business, and then I'll join you. We'll talk about our bright futures."

Nora rushed to her.

And that's when it hit me. By cracking this part of the case, I was driving Nora away. Because of me, she will be sent home.

I was sorry to see Nora leave.

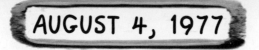

10:45 AM

This morning, I helped Nora and James carry their bags downstairs to a waiting taxi, which would take them to the airport. James was already inside the cab. Nora and I stood next to the passenger door.

"So . . . ," Nora started and her voice trailed off.

I had spent most of last night thinking about things. "So, I believe you. I don't think you were using me. At least not the whole time."

Nora's smile was like a bright bulb flashing to life. "San Francisco isn't so far from Hartland, Nebraska."

We both laughed, knowing we might never see each other again.

Her eyes were shiny with tears. "Will you write me?"

"Of course," I said, and I will.

She gave me a quick peck on the cheek and ducked into the taxi. I could hear her brother telling the driver that his hero was Kojak, the bald detective from TV. He sounded like he had embraced his baldness.

I didn't even have to look. I knew R.T. was standing behind me, making sure that I was okay.

As I watched the taxi drive away, my brother walked over next to me. "What are you going to do?"

I answered, "What we've been trained to do."

I realized that I'd gotten sidetracked and hadn't followed up the Histiaeus clue. I'd been wasting time with our silly plot to shave John's head. "We need to figure out what that clue really meant."

107

We headed back to our room to discuss the case.

"Let's get Judge involved," I said.

"Sure . . ." R.T. didn't sound convinced.

"What?"

"I mean that would be the right thing to do . . . ," said R.T.

"But you don't think we should."

R.T. shrugged. "Look, it's easy for you to say. Nora is gone. But I want to dance tonight. I'm the lead, bro. If we tell Judge, she's going to pull the plug on the whole thing and ship us back to Nebraska."

After a moment's thought, I nodded. "Okay. We'll keep quiet for now, but we tell her right after the show."

R.T. gave me a worried smile. "She's going to be mad."

I shuddered. I'd seen Judge when she was upset, and it wasn't pretty.

12:10 PM

The BIG SHOW is just hours away! Not only is it the last show, it's the one where Mrs. Craffin will be appearing to return the ankh necklace to the Egyptian authorities on live television.

Even though Judge knows the notes to Mrs. Craffin came from Nora, she is still concerned about security. So she changed Mrs. Craffin's routine and switched the guards around. Frank was replaced by another exhibition guard.

I watched R.T. during dress rehearsal. It looked like he finally had the incredible leap down. He could do it now without even a grunt of effort.

That's why it was so shocking when Madame Katerina stormed out on the stage.

"What are you doing?" she shouted at R.T.

R.T. made the incredible leap look easy!

"I'm sorry?" R.T. looked stunned.

"This is all wrong!" Madame Katerina announced angrily. "My Muse has made a special daytime visit and spoken to my head. All the dance must be changed!"

I wanted to suggest that someone who heard so many voices in her head might want to think about a visit to the doctor.

Madame Katerina must have sensed a pep talk was in order—either that or face mutiny from her dancers. "That old leap is for little children," she told R.T. and the others. "You are TEENS FOR TUT. You must dance like the great king! That nine-year-old king would have laughed at your silly efforts! You must jump farther and higher. Now watch as I show how new dance will be done."

"I . . . don't . . . know . . . if . . . ," R.T. started to say an hour later, but he was so out of breath, he couldn't finish. The two of us were running through the new dance steps on the empty stage again and again.

"Yes, you can do it. We just have to practice," I told him.

Just then, someone called my name. I turned to find Lucy holding out a letter to me.

"This just came for you," she said, and scurried off before I could thank her. I looked down at the envelope and the return address.

"Don't tell me it's already a note from Nora?" R.T. teased.

"I'm not sure," I said. I couldn't make out the postmark, and there was no return address.

"Why don't you take a break?" R.T. said. "Go back to our room and read your letter."

Once I was back in our room, I tore open the letter quickly, but I was disappointed to see that it was from King Richard. He was writing to me from his hospital bed.

> Dear Assistant,
>   Thanks for the code puzzle you sent to keep me busy while I recover. I think I cracked it.
>
> — King Richard

I smiled. Good for Richard. He'd cracked my code. My eyes continued down the page and suddenly, my heart started pounding as I read the rest.

P.S: To answer your question, yes, there was a hieroglyph on the floor next to me. I thought I might have been hallucinating. But your question sparked a memory. I saw a hand take it away. The symbol looked like this:

So there had been a hieroglyph!
I deciphered the hieroglyph. It said PORTA.
Porta . . . porta . . . porta . . . What could that mean?
I know of a famous cryptologist named Porta.

TEC TIP
SOUR EGGS

Mix together one ounce of alum and one pint of vinegar. Use the mixture to write a secret message on the shell. The mixture will disappear through the porous shell but show up on the hardened egg white inside. All the recipient has to do is peel off the shell to read the message! This clever trick was invented by sixteenth-century Italian scientist Giovanni Porta.

The egg!

I *thought* about the egg that R.T. had been about to eat on the bus. He had snuck it from somewhere, but I never found out where. Had he eaten it yet?

There was one way to find out.

I walked slowly to the mini refrigerator that we kept in our room.

The egg was still there. With a slightly trembling hand, I reached out and took the egg.

Just from the solid weight of it, I could tell it had been hardboiled.

I tapped the shell on the corner of the refrigerator, and a spiderweb of cracks appeared on its surface. Slowly, carefully, I peeled the shell from the egg.

I forced myself to remove the entire shell before examining the white surface of the hardened egg.

And sure enough, I found a message written there. It read:

FAIL AND PAY THE PRICE!

1:15 PM

Is the person sending these messages causing the accidents?

I wish I had someone to bounce ideas around with. But I decided to let R.T. keep rehearsing.

I opened up my notebook and started making a list of suspects. I listed the ones I could by last name first, thinking

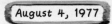

this would be a great way to treat each person more objectively. I decided I could rule out anyone who had suffered an accident. I guess they could have faked them, but it seemed unlikely.

Finally, I had to complete my list of possible suspects, and reluctantly added the last name.

MR. MYLES: A strong suspect. The "accidents" and the curse were great ways for him to build publicity. Plus, they were the only way that he could get rid of the people that he had signed contracts with.

MADAME KATERINA: She had wanted to fire Max and Carla—were the "accidents" her way of following her Muse?

MR. MYLES'S ASSISTANT: Lucy always seemed to be around.

FRANK THE SECURITY GUARD: Also always around when "accidents" occur.

MOORIE, R.T.

Suddenly, I flashed back to the faceless villain who kept appearing in my dreams about Sherlock Holmes. It was Moriarty. Had my code-breaking mind been solving the case the whole time? Had it been trying to tell me the answer to the mystery?

I wrote a new line:

MORIARTY = MOORIE, R.T.

Suddenly, everything made way too much sense, and images flashed through my mind. My brother telling me he would do anything to be the lead dancer. My brother pulling me back before I could try to save Carla. My brother daring Max to go outside on the skates . . .

Who would have the most to gain from all the accidents? The answer was obvious: R.T.

"No! That can't be!" I said out loud. But a voice in my head told me it was true.

Okay, take a breath, I told myself. Just suppose it was true. Why would R.T. leave hieroglyphs behind after the accidents? That didn't make sense.

But he would never have been lead dancer if Max had not sprained his ankle.

And he had sidetracked me from the Histaiaeus clue. Maybe R.T. had an accomplice, and they communicated by using the hieroglyphs.

Plus, R.T. had the egg.

Could my twin brother be the one behind all this?

No matter what, this egg could have something to do with Mrs. Craffin. She could be in danger. I have to tell Judge.

2:00 PM

I might as well tell the truth. It's been me this whole time. I'm the one who has been sending the hieroglyphic messages. Now that I have no fear of getting caught, I can tell the truth. I planned the whole caper by myself and pulled it off during the show. I sent the messages out to everyone in the world, and no one even realized it. I am the mastermind!

2:45 PM

My head . . . my head . . . is spinning!

I don't know who left that previous entry, but I surely didn't! Someone wrote it in my handwriting.

I was just finishing my entry, writing the words "I have to tell Judge," when someone put something over my nose and mouth, and I lost consciousness.

When I woke up, my head was resting on top of my journal. I flipped through it groggily, and that's when I discovered that the previous entry had been forged.

Someone was trying to frame me for the accidents and for a crime that will take place during the show!

 I looked at my watch. I must have woken up early, because the show had not even started yet. There was still time for me to stop whatever it was that was about to happen!

But who knows my handwriting? Who would want me out of the way?

The only person who could gain from something like this is my brother, R.T.

When I got to the stage, everyone was rushing about, preparing for the show. The live audience was being led to their seats.

Mrs. Craffin might be the target of the "caper" mentioned in the false journal entry. No matter what loyalty I have to my brother, I had to tell Mrs. Craffin to get out of the building.

But as I got close, I realized it was Judge— in disguise!

When she saw the recognition in my eyes, she held a finger to her lips, indicating I should speak quietly.

"Where's Mrs. Craffin?" I whispered.

Judge smiled and leaned closer to me so no one could overhear.

Judge disguised as Mrs. Craffin

"She is safe until she is to make her appearance. I wasn't feeling right about all the accidents lately and wanted to take some precautions, like switching the security guards around and wearing this disguise."

What a relief! Mrs. Craffin was out of danger. The urgency had been removed. I still had time to investigate and warn Judge before Mrs. Craffin made her appearance.

Judge's blue eyes were staring at me. "Are you all right, Zeke?"

What to do? Should I reveal what I thought my brother might be up to? That seemed wrong until I was sure of what was happening.

I plastered a big fake smile on my face, and hoped it looked a little convincing. "I'm fine. I just have to straighten something out."

Before Judge could say another word, I rushed off, looking for R.T.

I knew where I'd find him.

I went behind the curtain where the other dancers were warming up. But there was no sign of R.T. The floor lights had been plugged in, and as I watched their feet, I thought more about the forged entry in my journal, especially the line: "I sent the messages out to everyone in the world."

But how? On the TV show? How would you be able to send a message to the whole world without anyone on the show or in the audience or at home knowing it?

It wasn't like a telegraph system where I could just follow the wire that led from the sender to the receiver.

Or was it?

I watched the feet tapping on the dance floor.

Tapping.

And then it hit me—the dance floor!

Of course!

The dance floor served as a telegraph!

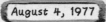

The dance floor was actually like a telegraph machine, and the feet of the dancers were like transmitters, tapping out messages.

While I was helping R.T. learn the latest dance, I had memorized the steps, and so I started to decode the pattern of the floor.

The message I uncovered knocked me to knees. I was trembling when the skinny chorus girl put her hand on my shoulder.

"Zeke? What is it?"

I couldn't answer her.

"My brother," I managed to say. "I have to find my brother and stop him—"

"Did you say your brother?" she asked, her eyes getting all dreamy. "Not that I'm watching him constantly or anything, but I just saw him."

"Where?" I asked.

She answered, "He went into the control room a few minutes ago."

Mr. Myles was unconscious!

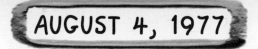

2:55 PM

I burst into the control room.

R.T. was there in full costume except for his mask, which sat on the counter behind him. He was standing next to Madame Katerina. They both looked up in shock. They were standing over the slumped body of Mr. Myles.

Chloroform sat on the desk in front of them.

"What did you do to Mr. Myles?" I demanded. "R.T., answer me."

R.T. looked stunned. "You don't think I did it, do you?"

There wasn't time to worry about his hurt feelings. "What happened to him?"

"Chloroform. He should be okay in about an hour," R.T. said. "Enigma . . . Zeke, you DO think I did it!"

"I just read the forged entry in my diary. I found your egg and the message written on it."

"What did it say?" Madame Katerina asked.

I glanced back at R.T. "I don't know," I told her. "It was written in Japanese."

Madame Katerina shook her head. "That's impossible—"

She clamped her mouth shut, and her eyes went wide. But it was too late. She had given herself away. R.T. was innocent. The villain was Madame Katerina!

"R.T., run!" I shouted and turned toward the door.

Madame Katerina spoke with such cold venom, she stopped me in my tracks. "Close the door. You're not going anywhere." Her Russian accent had completely disappeared.

When I looked at her again, she had pulled a short dagger out of her cane. She waved it in the air, motioning for me to do as she said.

After I closed the door, I turned back to her. "Who are you working for? Who is your MUSE?"

Madame Katerina said, "I don't know their real names. Only that they promised me buckets of money and a ticket out of here, out of this stupid job. I had no direct communication with them. They sent me the original key to send a message using the dance floor. That key had to remain the same no matter what."

"What messages have you been sending out?"

Madame Katerina shrugged. "Every night, Mr. Myles showed the Secret Map Box. Afterward, Frank locked the box back in its display case and used a new combination to lock the case. Then he wrote the combination inside the cover of the book he was reading. I would take a peek early the next day and change the choreography so that we were sending out the new combination to the lock. The robbers were supposed to get the combination and use it to steal the box."

"So why have you had to do this all more than once?"

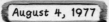

I asked. "Why didn't they just use the first combination you sent?"

Madame Katerina's expression turned to rage. "The messages kept going out garbled or incomplete. First, the lighting designer messed up the lights, then Carla mixed up the music and the dancers skipped some steps, and finally, Max couldn't do the dance needed to send out the message. And the people I work for got angrier and angrier. They would cause 'accidents' and leave me secret, coded messages. They are worried about being detected, so I had to use hieroglyphs to crack the code. But they all said pretty much the same thing.

Automatically, I said, "'Fail and pay the price.'"

Madame Katerina looked impressed. "That's right. And I'm not going to fail them again. But it won't be easy. Thanks to your friend Justine Pinkerton, the security guards have been switched. The new guard memorized the new combination and didn't write it down. So I don't know the new combination to unlock the display case. The dance tonight tells them that."

That didn't make sense to me. "But that will make them even angrier, won't it?"

Madame Katerina smiled. "I find honesty is the best policy, don't you?" She held out her hands like a small child who's been caught with cookie crumbs on her face. "The fact the guards were switched is not my fault. I know my employers are desperate to prevent anyone other themselves from opening that box. If they can't get to the Secret Map Box, they will not allow it to be unlocked. I imagine they will do the next best thing to keep the box from being opened."

Now it was all starting to come together. "They'll kidnap Mrs. Craffin tonight. The robbers will get the key from Mrs. Craffin and steal the box at some later point."

Madame Katerina nodded toward a black-and-white TV monitor. It showed a blurry view of the audience. She pointed at a woman in the crowd.

"There she is," Madame Katerina said with a wicked smile. She was pointing straight at Judge—but Madame Katerina thought she was indicating Mrs. Craffin.

I had to stall for time. "But why the floor? There must be an easier way to communicate?"

Once again, the rage flared on Madame Katerina's face. "It was easy, but who could have imagined there would be so many blunders? It was the ideal way of sending out messages to people who want to remain anonymous. There is no way to trace who is decoding the message. The show is being transmitted to homes all around the globe. The robbers could be in one of those homes or right here in the audience. This is the way my employers wanted it—complete anonymity."

"You wrote that phony entry in my journal."

"Did you like that? I've written one or two fake checks in my day, but I never knew I had such hidden talent as a forger. You will take the blame for all this. Or at least tie up the authorities with suspicions long enough for me to get away.

"No one will believe that I did that."

"Don't be so sure. After all, you were ready to blame your own twin brother."

Her smiled broadened when she could tell that hit a nerve. Score another point for Madame Katerina. I tried changing the direction of the conversation. "Why did you knock out Mr. Myles?"

Madame Katerina said, "I had to make sure that the right dance is performed tonight. I couldn't risk any more mistakes."

"What was the message that was hidden under hair?"

"Clever boy! That was the moldy bread. Scrape it away, and the message was right there."

"What did it say?"

Madame Katerina said, "Another threat warning me that if I fail in this mission I'll be sorry. And I don't plan on failing. I have to let the robbers know that I couldn't get the code." She turned to R.T. "Get your mask on and get ready to dance."

R.T. looked at her like she was crazy. "No way."

Madame Katerina gazed at her small dagger. She didn't move it any closer to either of us, but the threat was clear. "Why do you think I told you that long story? So that you would understand that I will do anything to finish this job. Now get ready to dance. You have no choice."

R.T.'s eyes blazed with determination. "Yes, I do," he said quietly. And in a flash he grabbed a rag lying on the desk—in that same instant I realized that this must be the same chloroform-soaked rag that was used to knock out Mr. Myles—and earlier in the evening, me!

"No!" Madame Katerina shouted as she swept the dagger toward him.

R.T. knocked himself out!

125

But R.T. already had the rag over his own face. In an instant, his legs buckled and he collapsed to the floor, his limp body lying next to Mr. Myles.

"That was stupid . . . STUPID!" Madame Katerina shouted, spittle flying from her lips.

"Actually, I think it was pretty smart. Now you can't use him to send out your message—"

I turned to the door. But once again, Madame Katerina stopped me. And this time, she didn't have to say a word. She just took a step closer to my brother. She looked down at him for a moment, then at the weapon in her hand, and finally at me. She raised her eyebrows at me as if we were playing a game of chess, and she was waiting for my next move.

"Not to worry, I'll let your brother go. But first you must take his place out on the dance floor."

I was too flabbergasted to speak. She wanted me to dance R.T.'s part?

"You know the choreography. You're the only one. It has to be you."

"What? You've seen me. I can't dance!"

"I think you can do more than you know."

This was ridiculous. She was completely out of her mind. I had to stall for time until someone came into the control booth or until the show started. "I can program the lights to do whatever you want."

"That's exactly my point. You're a smart boy. You can do whatever you set you your heart to—whatever must be done."

I said, "Please don't give me a pep talk."

She gave a bitter chuckle. "The message must come from the dancer. You will dance."

"No, that's something I'll never do," I fired back. "You wouldn't hurt him. Not really. You're not that evil."

With our eyes still locked, Madame Katerina shrugged. "Maybe you're right, and maybe you're not. Are you willing to take that chance?"

I didn't think it would be possible, but her voice took on a colder tone. "Either way, if my employers can't get Mrs. Craffin, I imagine they'll take someone else they use as a hostage. Hmm . . . whom else might they take? Looks like your brother isn't doing anything special right now.

"Here are your choices, little man. Option number one: Don't dance, and you endanger your brother. Option number two: Dance, and Mrs. Craffin is kidnapped, but your brother will remain unharmed. I'd say it's a simple choice. Now, you'd better get changed. We go the air in . . ." (she glanced at her watch)". . . in less than five minutes!"

What should I do?

If I dance, Judge, who is in disguise as Mrs. Craffin, will be kidnapped. If I don't dance, R.T. might be hurt!

I didn't know what to do. That's why it was so surprising to hear the words tumbling out of my mouth.

"Okay," I said. "I'll do it. I'll dance."

I couldn't believe I was taking R.T.'s place!

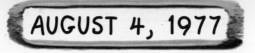
3:15 PM

With only a minute to go until show time, I left the control booth.

One of the boys in the chorus spotted me. He'd never bothered to speak to me before, but now he said, "You'd better hurry, dude."

He thought I was my brother. And why shouldn't he? I had switched clothes with R.T. and put on the mask.

I walked unsteadily out onstage and nearly tripped over my shoelace. If I couldn't even walk, how was I supposed to dance? Lucy caught me before I stumbled off the stage.

The mousy girl was surprisingly strong. "Two-minute warning, R.T." Then to the rest of the cast, she said, "Has anyone seen Mr. Myles?"

Lucy was looking toward the control booth. I couldn't let her go up there. Madame Katerina might panic and who knew what might happen then.

I lowered my voice to make myself sound like R.T. and hoped that the mask would muffle my voice. "Mr. Myles said you should call the show from down here."

She looked at me. For a minute, I thought she realized that I wasn't R.T. and was going to unmask me. But then she said, "Yes. I think I can do that."

I shuffled to where I thought R.T. started the show.

But I guess I was wrong, because the tall chorus girl gave me a little shove. "No, you stand over there. Are you all right?"

129

She started practicing the smaller leap the chorus did upstage when the lead dancer—who was now ME!—had to make his death-defying leap. It was clear she thought I was R.T. and was trying to impress me.

"Your shoe is untied," she told me as if she had just performed some invaluable service.

As the tall girl leaped back and forth in front of me, I kept scanning the crowd.

There! I spotted Judge in the audience. Her eyes were already on me, and her fingers were crossed as if to say, "Good luck!" She, too, thought I was R.T.

But in a flash, she frowned slightly. She did a double take, and I knew that even in this costume, I couldn't fool her. Her eyes ran over me, taking in the slimmer, shorter build. Her mouth formed the shape of a small O as she understood that I had taken R.T.'s place.

Looking a little worried, she started to get to her feet. I quickly raised a hand, signaling for her to stay seated. Judge hesitated then smiled slightly, shook her head, and sat back down. It was clear she thought R.T. and I were up to some kind of prank.

If only that were true!

I could feel the camera lens on me like the watchful eye of a hungry wolf. I'm sure Madame Katerina was watching my every move on the monitor.

She had told me as I left the control booth, "If you tell anyone what's going on before we start, I can't say what

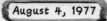

might happen to your brother."

Even now her words made my stomach clench with fear. I had to find a way to warn Judge without alerting Madame Katerina to what I was up to.

"We have to start," Lucy told the tall girl.

"Okay, let me do one more practice jump," the girl said.

Angling away from the camera, I crouched down to tie my shoe and waited for the girl to leap between the camera and me. When she did, she would block me from Madame Katerina's view for a moment and I could deliver a short message to Judge. Should it be "Run!" or "Danger!"? There wasn't enough time for me to decide—

Then the tall girl was running and jumping—and just as she passed between me and the camera lens—I twisted my mouth free from under the mask and mouthed the words: "de Bonet."

That's all I had time for. I jerked my face under the mask again and prayed that Judge would understand.

TEC TIP

HAND SIGNALS

Use sign language to send messages most people won't be able to read! In 1620, Juan Pablo de Bonet of Padua, Italy, published the first book that illustrated alphabet signs that could be made with the hands.

Judge's brow was furrowed in concern. Had she gotten the message? There was no more time.

"We go live in 3 . . . 2 . . ." The cameraman held up a finger, and the light on the camera suddenly glared red like the eye of a Cyclops.

A car salesman from Chicago was tonight's emcee, and he introduced the dance.

I was scared to death. My brother is the athlete, not me! I can't dance!

But I couldn't afford even a second of hesitation. My feet had to follow the moves of the dance exactly. Or my brother might be kidnapped or harmed—or both!

How strange that it was that the villain who ended up helping me find the inner strength I needed. Plus, the mask helped give me confidence. I could be anyone I wanted to be under here—and I realized then how much the way people treated you could affect your confidence. When people treat you like a star—like R.T.— you feel like a star.

My feet were going through the steps, lighting up the squares on the dance floor and sending a message out to the bad guys. I imagined each step that I took was a letter of the alphabet going out to the villains. That step was an O and that one a T.

Meanwhile, my hands were on their own mission. They were spelling out words to Judge.

"What are you doing with your hands? Stop it!" the tall dancer was hissing at me.

What could I say? I'm spelling words using my hands. I'm warning Judge that there is a kidnap plot and that my brother is danger. What are YOU doing?

But of course, I didn't say any of that. I had enough on my plate.

"Who are you?" the tall girl demanded as she spun close to me. "You're not R.T."

I felt like spinning this girl right offstage. I didn't need this now.

I risked a glance at Judge to make sure she understood. But she was gone. Her seat was empty! Either she had been kidnapped or she'd gotten my message and was headed for safety. But no matter what, I had to finish the dance.

I had managed to hit all the right steps, but there was still the big finale moment where I had to leap across the stage. Before I did, the choreography called for me to go behind the chorus dancers.

Breaking from the routine, the tall chorus girl ducked behind them with me.

"What are you doing?" I whispered to her.

"Who are you? What did you do to R.T.?" she hissed, and before I could stop her, she tore off my mask.

I did it!

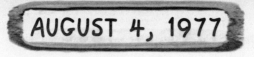

I reached for it, but she was backing away too quickly. I couldn't risk stepping on any unintended squares and sending out a garbled message.

The chorus dancers spread out to the sides of the stage, leaving me to do my solo leap.

Without the mask, I felt naked and exposed to the camera. I didn't have any protective layer. Now it was just I.

There was a slight gasp from the audience, but then they settled down, thinking this was all part of the show. The same couldn't be said for the other dancers. They seemed frozen in shock. "Not you!" one of them shouted. "You'll ruin everything!"

The tall girl's timing couldn't be worse.

I had to make the last big leap—the one that almost no one had been able to do before. I heard my brother's voice in my head, urging me on.

1 . . .

2 . . .

3 . . .

I felt myself break through that mental wall and—KABLAM!

4.

I did it!

I finished the dance! The crowd was on their feet.

I didn't take time to bow. Running off the stage, I headed to the control booth.

I threw open the door—

So frightened by what I would see—

And the first person I saw was Judge!

She smiled and rushed over to me. She gave me a hug. "Did you get it? Did you get my message?"

"Loud and clear, my friend," she hugged me harder. "The Secret Map Box and Mrs. Craffin are safe and sound. And so am I. Thanks to you."

When she pulled back, I could see a few security guards holding Madame Katerina between them.

"These men work for me," Judge said. "We'll hold onto her until the police arrive."

"The show—" Mr. Myles was waking up.

"R.T.?"

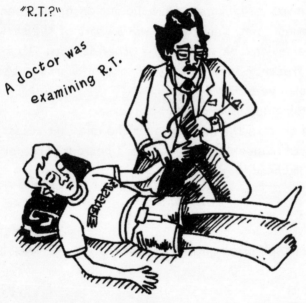

A doctor was examining R.T.

Judge looked across the room, and I followed her gaze. R.T. was still on the floor, but someone had placed a folded jacket beneath his head. A man with a stethoscope around his neck was holding R.T.'s wrist, checking his pulse. The doctor nodded at Judge. "He should be fine."

"But what about the robbers?" I asked her.

"See for yourself." Judge pointed to the far side of the exhibition space where two people were being led away in handcuffs. Even in their disguises, I recognized them. One was the man from the audience with the thick glasses that Max had landed on in New Orleans, and the other was the woman with the pearls who'd pushed me in Cincinnati.

The Vettles in handcuffs

Judge said, "Meet Dr. and Dr. Vettles. They are archaeologists who specialize in Egyptian art, but they are better known for stealing things from the digs they work on. Now, no one will allow them near a site. They were obviously desperate to take the box and its secrets for themselves, but the exhibition would not even let them examine it."

As she spoke, I remembered what Nora had said about uncovering an art fraud that involved the Vettles.

"The two of them concocted this whole scheme as a way to get their hands on the Secret Map Box before it could be decoded by the Egyptian government. They wanted to grab the hidden treasure for themselves. Thinking I was Mrs. Craffin, they tried to nab me when I headed backstage, but thanks to you, we were ready for them."

Judge patted my back as I hovered over R.T.

Lucy was operating the camera. Onscreen, a haggard but happy-looking Mr. Myles was accepting the ankh necklace from Mrs. Craffin. He looked tempted to hold onto the key, but he handed it over to the man from the Egyptian government.

R.T.'s eyes were still closed.

"Is he hurt? Is he okay?" I said to the doctor.

"I don't understand." The doctor didn't look as confident anymore. "He should have woken up by now."

"I think he already has," Judge said.

Suddenly, R.T.'s eyes opened. He rubbed at them lazily and then stretched as if he'd just been taking a nap. He sat up slowly, his hair rumpled on one side. "What? Can't a guy take a nap?"

He gave me a wink to let me know he was only kidding. "I could kind of hear what was going on." Then he said, "Way to go, Enigma. You're a real hero."

Laughing, I stuck out my hand and pulled him to his feet.

A NOTE FROM THE AUTHOR

Two of the greatest things I remember about the 1970s are disco roller-skating and the King Tut craze. When planning this book, I thought, "How cool would it be to combine those two things into one exciting mystery?"

In order to reach my goal, I had to reshape history a little. For instance, the King Tut exhibition of the 1970s didn't follow the path across the United States that I described. When it did stop in a city, it stayed longer than a week or two, as it does in my book.

Unfortunately, there probably wasn't disco dance extravaganza at the museum or a secret box that would unlock the unknown treasures of Tut. But wouldn't it be great if there were?

What is real in the book? Many of the investigative tools that Zeke uses to solve the crime are real, and so are all the cryptologists—like Porta—that help Zeke crack the case. If you are interested in codes, be sure to read more about these guys.

Just remember that Judge, the characters, and the story are about as real as my disco roller-skating talent. In other words, don't use this book when studying for a test. Or you might find your report card struck by the Curse of King Tut!

Yours in time,

Bill Doyle

ABOUT THE AUTHOR

Bill Doyle was born in Lansing, Michigan, and wrote his first mystery when he was eight. He loved seeing the shock on people's faces when they discovered the identity of the story's villain—and knew then that he was hooked on writing. Bill has written for Sesame Workshop, LeapFrog, Scholastic, ROLLING STONE, TIME FOR KIDS, and the Museum of Natural History. He lives in New York City with a mysterious dachshund named Esme.

HOW? WILL THE [ESO]...?

MORGANS → SAME FAMILY → WORLD'S TOP [SPIES]

FIND THE CODE! OR IS IT TOO LATE?

Check out these other gripping Crime Through Time™ books!

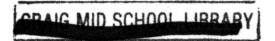